# Three Days to Angel Pass

Lucas Redwood makes wrong choices for the right reasons. A giant of a man, hardly aware of his own strength, he accidentally causes the death of a bullying lumber-camp foreman when he goes to the defence of a friend. Persuaded that the tyrannical boss will believe this was murder, Lucas decides to run. With no money to provide for his family, he becomes involved in a robbery which goes bad.

Set against the crucible heat of the Mojave Desert, in an industry where workers are cruelly exploited, how will Lucas's fellow workers react when they discover he is innocent? Will this flawed hero evade his pursuers and make it to the border crossing at Angel Pass?

# Three Days to Angel Pass

Rob Hill

A Black Horse Western

ROBERT HALE · LONDON

© Rob Hill 2011
First published in Great Britain 2012


ISBN 978-0-7090-9384-8

Robert Hale Limited
Clerkenwell House
Clerkenwell Green
London EC1R 0HT

www.halebooks.com

Typeset by
Derek Doyle & Associates, Shaw Heath
Printed and bound in Great Britain by
CPI Antony Rowe, Chippenham and Eastbourne

*for Val and Joss*

# 1

As Lucas Redwood sat outside his tent that morning, he had no idea that before daylight spread across the sky a man would lie dead and he would be on the run. For the moment though, he massaged spit and whetstone along the cutting edge of his axe blade in preparation for the coming day's work. It was the axe his father had earned his living by, brought from the old country and passed down to him. The beech shaft was polished by years of wear and the steel head was balanced and true.

Staring out over the desert from this vantage point, Lucas watched sunrise split the sky from the high peaks and morning light silhouette the mountains which crowned the playa. Amidst the cacti and mesquites on the far edge of the plain, he made out the swaying lamps of a mule train heading this way. This meant a collection of charcoal for delivery to the smelters on the other side of the mountains.

A little below where he was sitting amongst the rows of cutters' tents, four adobe brick, beehive shaped kilns stood in line each one the size of a house. Last year the date had been etched above the entrances while the mud was still wet, 1871. Beyond the kilns, a cottonwood shack doubled as company office and bunkhouse for the manager and foremen. Further down the slope, trestles and benches were set out in front of the chow tent.

Here and there oil lamps stood in pools of yellow light and murmured conversations ebbed in the cool air as men emerged from their tents. A breeze carried the smell of coffee and wood smoke and at any moment Lucas expected to hear the clang of the cook's triangle. Instead came the sound of voices raised in argument.

It was the usual argument. Charcoal production was down. The kilns were so big they could cope with more wood than the cutters could produce. The more timber the cutters felled, the further they had to walk to get to the forest's edge and the further they had to haul the timber back to the kilns. The ground rose steeply from here and when they asked for mules, the company refused to supply them. The foremen wanted to move the woodcutters' tents the half-mile up to the tree line, but there was no spring there which meant the men would have to carry water as well as supplies up the slope.

While the woodcutters were paid a daily rate, the foremen were paid a bonus against bushels of charcoal produced and transported by mule train to the smelting works. When the charcoal burners complained that they were having to fire half-empty kilns, the foremen could see their bonuses disappear. Formerly peaceful mornings now started with one or other of the foremen berating the leaders of the cutting teams, accusing them of being soft on the men, threatening to withhold their pay or to can them altogether. Added to this, while nights at this altitude were cold, the daytime sun turned the playa below them into a crucible and the forest where the men worked into a humid home for black gnats and mosquitoes. The mood in the camp was bitter.

Everyone understood that the foremen were under pressure from the company but the cutters resented being held responsible for the slow-down in production. A visit from John Gulliver was scheduled today. Gulliver was outright owner of the silver claims, the smelting works and had land rights to the mountain slopes where the charcoal production operation was sited. Nervous about having to face the boss with falling production figures, the foremen were even more bad tempered than usual.

The cook's triangle clanged. At once, men emerged from their tents holding their tin plates and cutlery and hurried down the slope to where rows of benches and trestles were set out. Lucas slipped his axe inside his tent and fell in with the tide of men moving down the hill. The smell of fried pork, beans and fresh baked bread was in the air. The sound of men arguing became louder.

Lucas was a giant of a man. Well over six feet tall, his torso was square and powerful. His steel biceps measured the circumference of an ordinary man's thigh. Because of his size and strength, other workers always wanted to count him as a friend so he had developed a calm and friendly manner; as people would always give way to him, he rarely needed to assert himself. He was proud of his strength. He enjoyed being called on to help out in situations that proved too much for other men and was content to work alone because none of the other cutters could keep up with him. If a job required partners, like using the great two-man saws, Lucas would take one end and a team of cutters would take turns at the other.

August Hobbs, manager of the charcoal camp, and Pablo Caborca, leader of one of the cutting teams faced each other on the porch to the company office. Usually,

Hobbs kept his distance from the men and communicated with them through the two foremen, but this morning – with the boss due – he was edgy and felt the need to stamp his authority. He always wore a gun-belt, which was out of place at a working camp and caused the men to laugh at him behind his back. Caborca was cousin to Lucas's wife. He had been given the team leader's job because he was hardworking and trustworthy but he was a quiet-mannered man unsuited to being in charge.

Hobbs barked accusations and his hand hacked the air between them while Caborca, embarrassed and humiliated, stared at the ground. Hobbs maintained Caborca's team was not cutting fast enough and was adamant he had seen him allowing his men breaks, whilst other teams were working, the previous day. He threatened to can him. As it was the argument the men had grown used to hearing, no one paid much notice as they filed past on their way to breakfast.

While the men knew threats like this were generally empty and could be safely ignored, they also knew that, as Hobbs was manager, he had to be treated with more caution than the foremen. In addition, they knew that with John Gulliver's imminent visit triggered by the fall in production, Hobbs would be desperate to prove himself to the boss. Caborca was an easy target. The men also knew that even for Hobbs to impress so hard bitten and powerful a man as Gulliver was nigh on impossible. They averted their eyes and hurried on towards breakfast.

As Lucas passed, Hobbs grabbed a fistful of Caborca's shirt and shook him. Both men were shouting now. Caborca pulled away as Hobbs clenched his other hand into a fist and raised his arm. Contempt twisted his face. Instinctively, Lucas darted towards them and clamped

10

Hobbs's wrist in his huge hand. With his free hand, Hobbs went for his gun. Lucas intended to knock the gun out of Hobbs's hand with a swipe of his other arm, but caught Hobbs on the jaw and sent him flying backwards against the corner of the foremen's shack. The Colt skidded across the porch. Whether it was the angle at which the back of his head hit the sharp corner, the nails protruding from the unplaned wood or the force of Lucas's blow which caused Hobbs to lie there without moving, no one could say.

A crowd gathered. Lucas leaned forward and hauled Hobbs to his feet. He stood there swaying slightly for a moment while his eyes refused to focus and words collapsed in his mouth. Then his legs buckled underneath him and he crumpled into a heap on the wooden floor of the porch. When Lucas reached for him a second time, dark blood oozed from a gash in the back of his head. He was dead.

Lucas and Caborca stepped back in horror. Realizing what had happened and that it was best not to see anything, the crowd quickly drifted away and joined the line outside the chow tent. Caborca looked around for the other foremen and spotted them eating breakfast at the trestle closest to where the cook served.

'Ain't your fault,' Caborca said. 'You never meant it.'

Lucas knelt beside the body and stared at the expression of surprise on the face. He felt for a pulse on the man's neck and looked up at Caborca.

'You got to get out of here,' Caborca whispered. 'This is the manager. They're gonna say you done it on purpose.'

The men had formed a chow line so it blocked the view of the table where the foremen were sitting.

'He had hold of you,' Lucas said.

11

'That don't matter now,' Caborca said. His face broke with worry. 'You got to get out of here right now. That line's gonna move and those foremen'll see him.'

'I'll explain,' Lucas said. 'I'll tell them.'

But he knew it was no good.

'They'll shoot you,' Caborca said. 'They got the boss comin'. Fellas like them are always desperate to impress the boss.'

The chow line seemed to be moving more slowly than usual. Lucas looked out across the dry lake bed. To the east, morning light thinned the indigo sky and silhouettes of trees and rock turned from shadow to substance. The mule train made its slow progress across the desert floor.

Lucas looked into Caborca's eyes. The Mexican smiled at him.

'Take the gun,' Caborca said.

Lucas had forgotten about Gulliver's Colt. He picked it up and stuffed it in his belt. Caborca glanced anxiously at the chow line which was starting to move again.

'No one saw nothing,' Caborca said. 'That should give you a head start.'

Lucas cut back through the lines of tents and snatched up his axe, his most precious possession, then quickly made his way round behind the company office and up the slope towards the tree line. He moved fast, kept low and found gullies and boulders to hide his path. He circled wide round the camp, across the shoulder of the hill away from any line of sight. Before starting to drop down towards the lake floor, he looked back. The chow line was gone and all the men were seated at trestles. The morning sun lit the sky and down on the playa a group of approaching horsemen kicked up a cloud of dust.

Although it was barely an hour since first light, the heat

12

of the sun was already in the air. To Lucas's right the land rose steeply to the tree line where the pinyon pines began; to his left the hillside ran down to the lake bed. Miles of grey sagebrush stretched ahead. A pocket mouse skittered up the path and threw up a little dust trail. To one side a ringtail moved in a patch of sage, ready to pounce. Lucas snatched up a stone and lobbed it into the brush and the startled cat sprang away.

It was ten miles to Ponderosa – the nearest settlement. There was a store there which traded in supplies and hardware, a saloon, forge, stable and a few bleached wooden buildings. Lucas had friends there.

Maybe someone had hidden the body. Maybe the foremen hadn't noticed. As he strode on, Lucas imagined the men setting out up the slopes from the camp as they did every morning. It wouldn't be long before they missed him, if they hadn't already.

Lucas had left the camp desperate to get away but with no idea of where he was headed. Now he began to think straight: he would head home first to warn Maria, then go on to Ponderosa to borrow a horse. He thought of Maria and the child, their tiny mud-baked house and the dried-up patch of land on the edge of the desert which flooded every spring and baked as hard as kiln fired clay every summer. It had been Maria's parents' place. They had tried to farm but conditions were so harsh they had been forced to travel into the desert to work as labourers for the bauxite company. Lucas quickened his pace. The thought of Maria waiting for him gladdened his heart.

'Where's Gus?'

'Having a shave to make himself look respectable for the boss.'

13

Bill Wheeling and Cole Tucker, the two foremen, snorted with laughter. They both knew what they thought of August Hobbs. He was the only lumber camp manager since the world began to walk around with a six gun strapped to his thigh and square heels on his boots. They sat at a table apart from the men, mopped up the last of their beans with hunks of sourdough and picked shreds of pork out of their teeth. The boss's visit was uppermost in their minds right then.

'Still don't know what he thinks he's going to prove by riding out here,' Wheeling said.

'Make us move the camp nearer the tree line,' Tucker said. 'That's all he can do.'

'The men won't like it.'

'Reckon he'll care about that?'

The men stood up from the trestles and made their way back to their tents to collect their gear. Without being asked, some of the teams were already starting up the slope towards the trees.

'We got one kiln half-full yesterday,' Tucker said. 'Got to get that sealed up before the boss comes.'

'Ain't like Gus to miss breakfast,' Wheeling said. 'He's always first in line.'

They caught each other's eye, another private joke. The two foremen got to their feet. Tucker nodded to the cook and told him to keep Hobbs's food for him.

Down on the plain, the dust-cloud thrown up by the group of horsemen was getting closer. The air was warm now, the sun had climbed into the porcelain sky.

Wheeling strolled over to the kilns to talk to the charcoal burners. It would look good if they could be unloading a kiln as the boss rode in. Tucker stood on the porch to the foreman's quarters and office and cast an eye

14

over the camp ready to call out to any stragglers. But unusually there were none. The last of the men were moving up the hill and he could already hear the regular chock of the cutters' axes at work above the tree line.

Where the hell was Gus?

Tucker stepped inside. The office was a single room with two bunks against the back wall and a folding canvas-bed beside them. An unlit oil lamp and a pack of playing cards stood on a table and three chairs were pushed underneath. Against a side wall was a locked safe, which the boss had insisted on providing. It had taken a train of six mules to haul it up there. It contained the payroll which the bank sent up under guard for distribution on the last day of the month and a ledger in which the daily production of charcoal was recorded.

The payroll had arrived yesterday and was due to be distributed this evening. But it was the record of production which the boss would want to see. Tucker wanted to go over it again before he got there. To have the figures in his head would look good. The problem was, there was only one key and that was attached to August Hobbs's belt. As manager, he had taken charge of it. Where the hell was he?

Tucker stepped out on to the porch again and shaded his eyes against the morning sun.

Wheeling laboured up the slope from the kilns.

'Told 'em to put off unloading till the boss gets here.'

He leaned against the corner of the wall to catch his breath.

'Boy, that hill gets steeper every day.'

'Seen Gus?' Tucker said. 'I wanted to look at the ledger.'

'Ain't seen him.'

15

Tucker continued to scan the camp. The dust-cloud thrown up by the horsemen had almost reached the edge of the lake bed.

'Reckon he's gone down to meet the boss?' Tucker said.

The men grinned at each other.

'Could have gone up into the woods,' Wheeling said. 'Make it look as though he was doin' something for once.'

They both laughed.

Tucker walked round the side of the shack and stared up towards the trees. The regular chock of the axes, the shouts of the men and the sound of splitting timber rolled down the hillside. He stepped further up the slope, still peering at the trees. Then something behind the office caught his eye and he cried out. Wheeling stumbled up to join him.

'What is it?' he said.

They both stared down at August Hobbs's body which lay behind the office wall with his hands folded neatly over its chest and his eyes closed as peacefully as if he were asleep.

'Well, wake him up,' Wheeling said.

Then he realized. He took a step backwards and grabbed at the wall to support himself.

Tucker stooped and felt for a pulse. He looked up at Wheeling.

'The key,' Wheeling said.

Hobbs's belt ran through an iron ring which held the safe key. The men looked at each other. The key rattled against Hobbs's belt buckle as Tucker unfastened it.

'I wanted to look at the ledger,' he said.

They stepped quickly round to the office door. The key clicked against the metal as Tucker found the lock. The safe door swung open on oiled hinges. There was the

16

ledger, some record books and alongside was a blue canvass bag with the bank's name stenciled in black capitals, tied at the neck and sealed with wax. It was stuffed with cash. Tucker glanced at Wheeling.

'Never get another chance,' he hissed.

Hoof beats sounded outside. A group of riders entered the camp. The charcoal burners had just started to unload one of the kilns. The riders dismounted and led their horses up the slope. The group was led by an older man, clearly in charge. Silver hair cascaded from under his black hat. A lace tie was at his throat and twin Colts were visible under his jacket. As Tucker and Wheeling emerged from the doorway of the wooden office, he raised his hand to greet them. His dark eyes were watchful and his face unsmiling.

'Fine morning boys,' he called. 'Where's Gus?'

# 2

Maria knew it was Lucas when he was still a mile away. He was striding fast with his axe over his shoulder. The heat of the day was beginning to gather so she went out to the well and lowered the old leather bucket. Lucas would be thirsty when he arrived.

Maria's black hair was tied in a single loose plait. Her handsome, broad-cheeked face was kind and determination born of the fight for survival showed in the set of her jaw. Laugh lines were ready around her mouth and her brown eyes missed nothing. She wore a white blouse over a wide embroidered belt and a blue cotton skirt on which she had sewn pockets. Her arms and shoulders were strong and she moved with easy confidence.

Outside the mud brick house, a roof of vines shaded a wooden table and chairs. A few tomatoes and a knife were on a plate in the centre of the table beside a handful of white beans soaking in a tin bowl. Chickens pecked in the dust, a she-goat was tied to a pole close to the well and a burro stood tethered beneath the fig tree. Beside the door, shaded by the vines was a rush basket in which a baby lay asleep.

Maria put the bucket down beside one of the chairs and

went into the house, glancing at the baby as she passed. She came out a minute later with a thin towel and hung it over the back of one of the chairs and sat down to watch Lucas approach. It was the last day of the month, maybe he had taken his pay and quit. Maybe he had been fired. It didn't matter. At least he had worked a full month. He waved and called out to her as he got closer. Maria stood up to greet him and glanced again at the baby whose head of black curls peeped above a white cotton sheet.

Lucas quickened his pace when he saw Maria. He propped the axe against the wall, flung his massive arms around her and held her tight against him. Her body melted into his. When he held her like this and buried his face in her hair and kissed her neck, love engulfed her, this was the safest place in the world and worry did not exist. But not this time, the Colt in his belt jabbed her in the ribs. Lucas had never owned a gun like this.

Lucas pushed Maria gently away and crouched down beside the basket where the baby lay. He reached out to touch the cheek of the sleeping child and Maria rested her hand on his shoulder. Lucas looked up at her.

'He's well?'

She smiled at him.

'Of course.'

Lucas noticed the bucket of water at his feet. He scooped out handfuls and rubbed it in his face and round the back of his neck. Then he drank from his cupped hands and laughed as silver water splashed between his fingers. He snatched the towel Maria had left ready for him and dried his face. As he turned to her, his smile faded.

'Got trouble comin',' he said.

Lucas looked into her brown eyes and told her every-

19

thing. He told her about how the manager had picked on Pablo Caborca, how he had yelled in his face and twisted his shirt tight to his throat. He explained how the foremen always said they had to work faster, take less breaks and made them work until after dusk. But mostly he told her about when Hobbs hit his head on the corner of the office building it had hardly made any sound at all and when Lucas yanked him to his feet, he was surprised when he stumbled and fell a second time. He said he didn't really believe that Hobbs was dead until Caborca insisted he take the gun.

Maria stood behind Lucas and massaged his shoulders. She stared out across the desert, past the well and the burro and the fig tree into the miles of dust and cacti and sagebrush as if she expected more riders to appear at any moment. Then she looked down at the baby who slept through everything.

'Do they know where this place is?'

'They'll find out.'

'But they'll know you didn't mean it,' Maria said. 'Caborca and the other men will speak for you.'

'It was the manager,' Lucas said. 'Won't make no difference.'

'Maybe you shouldn't have taken the gun.'

Lucas looked at her.

Maria stopped massaging his shoulders and walked round the side of the house to where a shallow fire pit was dug for cooking. She came back with flat tortillas and set them on the table in front of Lucas. The smell of new baking hung in the air. Maria disappeared into the house for a moment and came out with a dish of honeycomb and a cup for water. She sat down opposite Lucas and watched him eat.

'You'll have to go away for a while,' Maria said.

'Ain't safe for any of us,' Lucas said. 'It was the manager.'

He looked towards the sleeping child.

'We'll go to my village,' Maria said quickly. 'Across the border. They can't reach us there.'

Lucas broke off another piece of bread and dipped it in the honey.

'I'll take the burro and bring the child,' Maria went on. 'You go on ahead. Hide out somewhere and we'll cross together. You'll have to wait for me. If you cross by yourself and someone sees a white man on his own, they'll think you've come to steal horses. You'll be fine if you wait for me.'

'We've got a few days,' Lucas said. 'Caborca and the others won't tell them nothing.'

Maria looked down at the child in the basket.

'We should start now. It's three days to Angel Pass.'

Lucas dipped the cup into the well bucket and drank. He pushed his chair back, strode over to a tilled patch of ground where tomato plants grew and began to search for fruit amongst the leaves. Out of the shade of the vines, the heat hammered down.

'Best wait till this evening,' Lucas said. 'There may be a breeze.'

He took off his hat and filled it with hard green fruit.

'I could take the goat in to Ponderosa,' Lucas said. 'Might get something for her. And I'll borrow a horse from the stables.'

'I'll take the chickens,' Maria said. 'If anyone stops me I'll say I'm going home because my father is sick. They'll believe me if it looks like I'm taking presents.'

Maria fetched a crock of corn flour, a flask of water and

21

the smooth stone for rolling out tortillas and set them down on the table. Lucas went into the house and bundled together their few possessions, took down the shotgun from its place on the wall and found the box of shells.

'There's a cantina at Angel Pass,' Maria called. 'You could meet me there.'

Her quick movements made the stone in her hand seem weightless as she prepared the neat flour discs.

'Travelling alone could be dangerous for you,' Lucas said.

'If someone sees us together, that puts the child in danger,' Maria said quickly.

She stared down at the dough and worked it hard under the stone.

'Anyway, I'll take the shotgun.'

The baby stirred in the basket. He raised up a tiny arm from under the sheet and with his eyes still glued, coughed as softly a kitten. They both looked towards him.

'He always wakes around this time,' Maria said.

It took an hour to assemble the men. Called away from the work they had just started and made to troop back down the hill to the camp they had just left, they were in a sour mood. When they saw John Gulliver scowling at them from the porch of the office, they weren't surprised. The boss was an autocrat. If he decided he wanted them to stop work so he could speak to them, that's what would happen. And if he decided to speak to them, it was never good news. Wheeling and Tucker ordered each man to stand outside his tent while they walked up and down the rows to see if anyone was missing.

'There's been a killing,' Gulliver announced. 'Gus

Hobbs had the back of his head stove in.'

The men fell silent.

'Happened this morning. When I got here, he was still warm.'

Gulliver looked out over the heads of the men. Rags of mist clung to the pines. 'Hobbs was a good man,' Gulliver announced. 'Some coward came at him from behind.'

He paused and looked into the faces of the men.

'Broke into the company office, opened the safe with the key from Hobbs' belt and took the pay roll.'

The men turned to each other.

'Now somebody here knows what went on. This happened right in this camp this morning.'

Gulliver paused. One by one he turned his eyes on the faces of the men and one by one they avoided his gaze.

'It's your money that's been took,' Gulliver said. 'Anyone willing to step forward?'

Gulliver waited. He pushed back his jacket and rested his right hand on the handle of his Colt.

'If there ain't no payroll,' he sneered, 'there ain't no pay.'

Conversation broke out amongst the men then.

'We don't get paid, we don't work,' someone shouted.

Gulliver laughed.

There was a disturbance from amongst the row of tents. Tucker shouted. The two foremen came running.

'Someone's missing,' Tucker said, catching his breath. 'That big fella, Lucas. He ain't here.'

Wheeling was standing next to the boss.

'Anyone seen Lucas?' he shouted.

No one caught his eye. The men turned to each other.

'There's your guilty man,' Gulliver called. 'Killed a man from behind, took the wages of his fellow workers and run off like the coward he is.'

23

'I'll search inside his tent,' Wheeling said, barely able to contain his excitement. 'He might have got the money stashed.'

'Sir,' one of the men approached Gulliver. It was Pablo Caborca. He held his hat in his hands. 'Lucas never done this. He never hurt nobody. He ain't got it in him.'

Gulliver stared at him.

'You a friend of his?' Gulliver snapped.

Caborca nervously twisted the brim of his hat.

'Where do you think he might have gone?' Gulliver continued.

'Sir, I. . . .'

'Where does he live? Does he come from round here?'

'I just know Lucas couldn't have done nothing like this,' Caborca said.

Gulliver pushed Caborca aside.

'I want a posse,' Gulliver shouted. 'Ten men. Good riders. The rest of you get back to work.'

Wheeling scampered into Lucas's tent on all fours. There was a bed-roll and a lamp. His axe was missing. Wheeling pulled the bed-roll aside. A flat stone lay under where Lucas would have rested his head. This was where all the men stashed their money. Levering up with his fingers, Wheeling pulled out a leather purse tied with a draw string. He could hear the voices of the men outside the tent. He pulled open the purse. A few folded bills, the previous month's wages.

'Whatcha doing in there, Wheeling?' someone called. 'Gone to sleep?'

Wheeling stuffed the money into his pocket, shoved the purse back under the stone and pulled the bed-roll over it.

'Nothing here,' Wheeling shouted and crawled backwards out of the tent.

*

Half an hour later, the horsemen fanned out across the hillside. The air was already hot and by early afternoon the sun would use the playa as an anvil. Gulliver shaded his eyes and scanned the lake bed.

'Could have climbed up above the tree line,' Wheeling suggested, seeing an opportunity to get up amongst the pines where the air was cooler. 'He'd know we couldn't see him from down here.'

Gulliver considered.

'We'll split up. You take five men and search the trees. Me and Tucker'll take the rest and head down to Ponderosa. If you find him, keep him alive. If you ain't come across him in a couple of hours, get back down here. I'm leaving you in charge of the camp.'

The Ponderosa saloon was empty apart from a man dozing on the porch with his hat over his face and his feet on the rail. Gulliver kicked the leg of the man's chair and he woke with a start. This was Charlie Decanes, the owner.

'Lookin' for someone,' Gulliver announced. 'Might have passed through here today.'

He described Lucas and mentioned his name. Charlie stood up. He knew Lucas well. Before he started work up at the charcoal camp, Lucas helped repair the saloon furniture after a pair of young drifters smashed up the place one night when the sheriff was out of town. He wouldn't take a cent for it.

'What did you say his name was?' Charlie said.

Irritation sounded in Gulliver's voice.

'You couldn't miss him. Big built fella.'

Charlie shrugged.

'What you after him for anyway?'

Gulliver's eyes were as dark and hard as jet.

'He killed a man and stole the payroll.'

Charlie whistled through his teeth.

'You boys want a drink?'

'Sure you ain't seen him?' Gulliver said.

Charlie took in Gulliver's new-looking hat, expensive pair of Colts and short-tempered manner. He shrugged again.

'Know it if I had.'

Things were much the same at the stable. As the heat of the day was building, old Buck Williams was asleep on a pile of hay and snoring gently. The family of mice which played around him skittered back under the straw when Gulliver strode in and nudged him with the toe of his boot. Williams sat up sharply with a series of adenoidal grunts. He pushed himself to his feet.

'Bringing in horses?'

'Looking for someone,' Gulliver said.

He described Lucas again and mentioned his name.

'Seen him in town today?'

Buck Williams rubbed his whiskers.

'Who wants to know?'

'I'm John Gulliver.'

'Owns the silver company?' Buck said.

Gulliver took a fold of bills from the inside pocket of his jacket and peeled one off. Buck's eyes fell on the money.

'What do you want him for?'

'Have you seen him?'

Gulliver replaced the fold in his pocket but kept the single bill in his hand. Williams tore his eyes away from the greenback and looked up at Gulliver.

'Can't say I have.'

'Know where he lives?'

Buck's whiskered face creased into a smile and he held out his hand.

'Somewhere north of town,' he said. 'Can't say exactly.'

Gulliver pressed the dollar into Buck's hand. He turned and the men followed him out into the sunlight.

# 3

Lucas pulled his hat down low and tugged the length of twine to hurry the goat. She was a good milker, he would start by asking five bucks for her. The heat of the day concussed him and the reflection of sunlight from the desert sand burned his eyes. A lizard scampered ahead of him and left a shallow trail in the dirt.

A man waved to him and shouted a greeting as Lucas passed a farmstead just like his own, a low mud brick building with a doorway shaded by vines. The gnarled branches of an olive tree reached over the roof and thin tomato plants climbed along a side wall. Some distance away was a corn patch where heavy cobs showed through the dark green leaves. Lucas waved back but kept going.

The heat filled Lucas's legs with lead, hammered inside his skull and glazed his face with sweat. His lips were paper dry. Eventually, as the land fell away, he saw the few ramshackle buildings which made up Ponderosa. From here they were the size of matchboxes. The sun had bleached the walls and roofs until they were the colour of the desert floor.

Lucas stopped dead. There was a group of horsemen in the main street preparing to leave. How had they tracked

28

him here so quickly? They would have asked for him in the saloon. Would Charlie have told them where he lived? There was no place for Maria to hide. He should have warned her, should have stayed with her. What difference would a few dollars for the goat make? He shaded his eyes and watched the men mount up. Six of them. Gulliver was out in front. He couldn't recognize the others from here. Then a miracle happened. At the end of the street, the riders headed north into the desert, the opposite direction to his farm.

'Bigity fella woke me up.' Buck was indignant. 'Kicked me while I was napping, if you please.'

Buck followed Lucas into the saloon.

'That was Gulliver,' Charlie said. 'Boss of the silver claims and just about everything else around here.'

He pushed a pitcher of water and two glasses across the bar. A quartered lemon bobbed on the surface.

'Said some things about you.'

Charlie looked at Lucas.

'Knew they weren't true,' Charlie went on. 'Said you killed a man and stole the payroll. Told him you never would have done nothing like that.'

'The payroll?' Lucas said.

Charlie poured water and the men and listened while Lucas explained what had happened. When he had finished Charlie whistled softly through his teeth.

'Reckon Caborca stole the money?'

'I got to sit down,' Lucas said.

He picked up his glass of water and pulled a chair from under the nearest table.

'Pablo wouldn't never steal the payroll. No one would,' Lucas said. 'The guys know each other. Some of them have

29

worked together for years.'

'Bad apples in every barrel,' Buck cautioned.

Lucas shook his head.

'Who was it then?' Charlie said.

'Maybe there wasn't no payroll,' Buck said. 'That Gulliver fella is trying to say someone stole it and there wasn't one in the first place. Then he'd have a reason for not paying the guys.'

'Wouldn't be the first boss to pull something like that,' Charlie said.

'The payroll was delivered yesterday, same as always,' Lucas said. 'Everyone saw it.'

Lucas drained his glass and poured another. He fished out the lemon with his fingers. The sour flesh stung his lips.

'It ain't all bad,' Buck said. 'He asked me where you lived. I told him north and he gave me a dollar.'

The men laughed.

'I reckon you want one of us to buy your goat because you're going to high tail it out of here,' Buck said. 'That's what you brung her for, ain't it?'

Lucas smiled.

'I ain't got no money but tell you what I'll do,' Buck said. 'I'll look after the goat and you can have her back when this is blowed over.'

'She's a good milker,' Lucas said. 'Worth five bucks, I reckon. What about you, Charlie?'

Charlie considered.

'I'll give you two bucks,' he said. 'That's your wages against next time I need repair work done. And I'll look after the goat and you can have her back when you're good and ready.'

'You can have my dollar I got from Gulliver,' Buck said.

'Reckon you'll be wantin' to borrow a horse too.'

He reached in his pocket and passed the bill over. Charlie went behind the bar and came back with two bills.

'Where are you headed?' Charlie said.

The sunlight was fierce in the dusty street. Lucas stared out through the doorway.

'Gulliver will come back,' Lucas said. 'He won't ask you nice a second time.'

Buck snorted. 'I'm just the old timer who sweeps out the stable.'

'Best if I don't say where I'm headed,' Lucas insisted.

'Won't get far on three dollars,' Buck said.

Lucas frowned. He pushed his chair back and got to his feet. He leaned down and patted the goat.

'Thank you, guys.'

'Only one horse in the stable, you can saddle her up yourself,' Buck said.

Lucas looked from one to the other of them. He pulled his hat down against the sunlight again and stepped out into the street.

A young man was tying the reins of his horse to the rail. He was lightly built and his movements were quick. The bones shone in his face and his blue eyes were cold as a sharpshooter's. Lucas didn't recognize him. His saddle was expensive and there were Colts in his gun-belt.

'Hot day,' the man said.

Lucas nodded.

'If you don't mind me sayin', you must be one of the tallest fellas I've ever seen. One of the strongest too.'

'Could be,' Lucas said.

He looked away, not wishing to be drawn into conversation.

'I'd like to buy you a drink,' the man persisted. He

31

smiled openly. 'Been riding all morning, ain't spoke to a soul.'

He was sizing Lucas up, looking at the way he held himself, judging the strength of his arms. He noticed the gun in Lucas's belt.

'Just leaving,' Lucas said.

He started down to the livery stable.

'But thanks.'

Lucas felt the stranger's eyes on him as he headed down the street. Later, when he had ridden past the edge of town he looked back, the man had disappeared into the saloon.

Three dollars. Would Pablo Caborca think to look in Lucas's tent for his stash of money? Would he think of bringing it to him? If he hadn't been so concerned with collecting his precious axe, he would have remembered it himself. The sun hammered down. Lucas scanned the horizon away to the north in search of the riders but there was no one, just sagebrush, cacti and the blinding reflection of the sun off the desert floor.

A mile after the climb out of town, Lucas dismounted at a thicket of mesquites which shaded a pool of clear water. Here a spring fed by one of the underground rivers broke through the desert crust. Lucas slumped down against a tree trunk while his horse drank. A coachwhip snake uncoiled itself from a branch on the opposite edge of the pool, slithered down the trunk and away amongst the rocks, its black head gleaming like tar. Lucas took off his hat, fanned his face, leaned his head back and closed his eyes.

It could have been a minute later or half an hour, Lucas heard hoof beats. His horse stood obediently at the edge of the pool. A turkey vulture circled above him. Lucas grabbed the pistol from his belt and pushed through the thicket for a view of the trail. A lone rider followed the path he had just taken. As he got closer, Lucas recognized the stranger who had spoken to him outside the saloon.

A few yards short of the mesquites, the rider reined in his horse and jumped down from the saddle.

'Anyone there?'

Holding the reins in one hand, the man spread his arms wide. Smiling in the same open way as he had outside the saloon, he stepped towards the thicket. His Colts glinted in their holsters. Lucas, still with his gun in his hand, pushed through the bushes and faced him.

'No need for guns, mister.'

The man stepped backwards and held up his hands, palms outwards.

Lucas noticed his expensive boots and holsters.

'You following me?'

Lucas stuck the Colt back in his belt.

'They told me in the saloon you was headed north. I saw you head south with my own eyes. We gonna stand here in the heat or take some shade under the mesquites?'

The men pushed through the brush and sat down by the edge of the pool.

'Asked you to have a drink with me earlier. Now we're having one,' the man said pleasantly.

He offered Lucas a handshake.

'John Gulliver junior.'

Lucas snatched the pistol out of his belt.

'I ain't going with you.'

Lucas got to his feet.

'No need to be jumpy, friend. I don't even know your name. First time I set eyes on you was back at the saloon.'

'What?'

33

The man smiled his open smile and lowered his voice.

'I want to make you an offer.'

Lucas backed away, still covering John Gulliver with his Colt.

'Chance to make some money. Put your gun down.'

Lucas sat down and leaned against the trunk of a tree again and kept Gulliver junior covered.

'I'm listening.'

'It ain't nothing illegal, we just got to keep it quiet,' Gulliver said. 'Nobody knows about it and nobody will unless you tell 'em. That's the beauty of it.'

He leaned forward and scooped a handful of water out of the pool. Then he looked at Lucas.

'I asked about you in the saloon. Those old guys in there claimed they didn't know you. Said you was a drifter and they'd never seen you before. I knew right off they was lying. You ain't no drifter. You ain't carrying no bed-roll, no possessions of any kind. You're from round here, just come into town for some reason. Any fool can see that. They said you was heading north.'

Gulliver junior laughed.

'Took a look through the saloon door and there you was, heading south.'

'What makes you so interested in me?'

'Those old guys was covering for you.' Gulliver junior was suddenly serious. 'You're in some kind of trouble, my friend.'

'I've heard enough,' Lucas snapped.

'Wait,' Gulliver junior said. 'I mean it. I've got a way we can both be rich.'

'You are rich.'

Gulliver laughed.

'I got debts at every gambling house on the coast. I got

posses of hoodlums looking to break my arms and my legs. If I set foot in San Francisco, I'll be shot on sight. If my father ever finds out there's a good chance he'll disown me and that's after he has me bull whipped.'

He stared at the ground. A spiny lizard darted out from behind a rock and scuffled away the dirt at his feet in search of insect prey. The rusty sound of cicadas rose in the air. Gulliver looked up at Lucas.

'I'm in trouble. We're the same, you and me.'

'You're nothing like me,' Lucas said.

The lizard froze for a moment then skittered back behind the rock.

'We can help each other,' Gulliver persisted.

Lucas shoved the pistol back in his belt and sat down again.

'I'm listenin',' he said.


Nine miles north of Ponderosa, Gulliver senior's posse rode hard. Ahead of them the air shimmered. The land here was a carpet of rattlesnake weed, their horses stamped the juicy leaves and tiny white flowers into the desert floor. At the edge of all living things, where the land was too dry and salty even for beaver tail cactus, they came upon a lone rider, a Mexican on a donkey cradling a pannier of gopher snakes. From a distance, Gulliver had assumed it was Lucas. When the Mexican insisted no rider had passed this way, anger lit in Gulliver's veins.

'If he'd come north we would have found him by now,' Gulliver snapped.

'We ought to rest the horses,' Tucker said. 'In this heat. . . .'

Gulliver glared at him.

'We turn round now. We've lost time.'

35

Up ahead, the horizon danced as the air melted and brown rock and dry salt beds stretched for mile after mile. The men were already ashen faced and sick with the heat. Gulliver jerked the reins of his horse and wheeled the animal to face the way it had come.

'That fella in the stable took my money and made fools out of us,' Gulliver announced.

The men glanced at each other.

'What do you want to do, boss?' Tucker said.

Gulliver scowled.

'Get back to that one horse town and try some other direction. We'll call in at the stable first.'

The burro stood patiently in the shade of the fig tree, while Maria finished tying the food basket, their clothes and few possessions on to the saddle. How much would Lucas get for the goat? A few dollars, that was all. Maybe she should stay. Lucas could go off and find work in one of the mines or even as far as San Francisco. He could come and visit her and bring her money and she would look after the child and everything would be fine.

Maria knew it couldn't be like that. If a boss was dead, they would blame a worker; neither she nor Lucas's friends had the power to protect him. She let her eyes wander over the little house that her parents had built with their own hands. She looked at the fig tree they had planted, the patch of corn Lucas had sown and the dirt where her chickens had scratched. Last of all she looked at the child, still sleeping in the basket under the shade of the vines. She had no choice. If she stayed, the child would be in harm's way.

The blazing heat of the day had passed but the sun was still high. Lucas should be home soon. She walked round the side of the house to scan the horizon. There was no sign of him yet, just sagebrush and cacti, the hot wavering air and the empty land.

## 4

'Wagon takes the silver ingots from the smelter down the valley to the Plataville rail-head,' Gulliver junior explained. 'Mile and a half if that. One driver, one shotgun.'

His ice-blue eyes studied Lucas.

'The security boys wait down at the rail-head. Ten men, all armed. They guard the loading and travel with the silver to San Francisco.'

Gulliver junior smiled as if he was passing the time of day and watched for Lucas's reaction.

'Company figured if they was going to be robbed, it would be when the train was being unloaded or when the silver was being taken to the bank, not out here.'

'That's your plan?' Lucas said. 'To rob the train?'

'The wagon,' Gulliver said. 'Before it gets to the rail-head.'

Lucas shook his head.

'Two thousand dollars worth of silver on that wagon,' Gulliver junior said.

Lucas studied the lizard tracks in the dirt at his feet.

'I'm in charge while my pa's away,' Gulliver junior went on. 'I give you the job driving the wagon. First day you're there, we do it, before the men have got time to know you.'

'No one gets hurt?' Lucas said.

Gulliver spread his arms wide and smiled his big open smile.

'There's a hairpin in the track down through the gully where the wagon is out of sight of the camp and the rail head. I'll leave a couple of horses there for you. One for you, other for the silver. You stop the wagon, unload and ride off. When the guys down at the rail-head realize something's wrong, they can't follow you because they've never even seen you.'

'Why are you askin' me?'

Gulliver laughed.

'Obvious, ain't it? You're strong. The silver is heavy. You've got to be real quick with the unloading otherwise the guys at the rail head will wonder what the problem is and ride out. And nobody knows you.'

'What about the driver?'

'What about him? I'll tell him he ain't needed on that journey. I'll find something else for him to do that morning. He's an old guy, worked there for years. He won't say nothin'.'

The heat of the day had passed. The rattle of cicadas in the leaves above the men quietened for a moment. A blue-bodied damselfly landed on the surface of the pool, opened its wings to the sun, stood there for a moment and then took off.

'Nobody knows you,' Gulliver repeated. 'And nobody will suspect me.'

'We meet up later?' Lucas said.

'Know Red Tail? There's an empty saloon building beside the old mineshaft. No one's been out there for years. That's where the guy I'm selling the silver to will meet us. He'll hand over the money. You'll take your share and we'll never see each other again.'

'There's one thing,' Lucas said. 'Your pa knows what I look like. I used to be a cutter for him.'

'He's up at the charcoal camp,' Gulliver said. 'Be back the day after tomorrow.'

'Then we got to do it tomorrow,' Lucas said. 'That bullion cart leave every morning?'

Gulliver junior smiled his big cradle smile. His blue eyes were cold.

'First light.'

They shook on the deal, Gulliver's gambler's fingers in Lucas's huge woodcutter's hand.

'I thought you'd forgotten your old woman.'

Maria reached up and flung her strong arms around Lucas' neck. He pulled her body to him, kissed her face again and again and held her. He loved this feeling of his arms wrapped around her.

'You ain't old,' Lucas said. 'And if you was, I'd be old along with you.'

He released her, gently smoothed her cheek with his hand and looked down to where the child stared at him from its basket. Bubbles of delight formed at the corners of the child's mouth. As Lucas reached down, the child grasped his finger with one tiny hand, his brown eyes shone at the sight of Lucas's smiling face and he laughed lightly. Lucas felt Maria's hand rest on his shoulder.

'You best be going.'

Lucas tore his gaze away from the child.

'Got the shotgun?' he said.

Maria kissed him.

'Angel Pass in three days,' she said. 'I'll wait for you.'

Lucas pulled the three dollars out of his pocket and handed them to her.

'Got a day's work tomorrow,' he said. 'I'll have more when I see you.'

Maria smiled.

'They taken you back woodcutting?'

'They'll be coming after me for what happened at the camp,' Lucas said. 'Ain't safe here now.'

Maria picked up the child's basket and handed it to Lucas.

'Pass him up to me.'

She climbed up on to the burro and pulled a blanket round her shoulders. Lucas passed her the basket. The child giggled playfully. She fixed the handles of the basket over the saddle horn. The shotgun rested across her knees.

'This work,' Maria said. 'Is it dangerous?'

'Driving a wagon,' Lucas said. 'Don't worry.'

Maria looked at him but didn't smile.

It was dusk now. Soon the moon would rise and stars would blanket the sky. Maria urged the burro forward. Lucas watched them until their shadows were swallowed by the darkness. He collected the food Maria had left for him, tied his axe to the saddle and headed out towards the smelting works. He would find somewhere to bed down for a few hours when he was well away from the house. For all he knew, Gulliver senior was on his way here now.

'Where is the old fool?' Gulliver senior snarled.

He jumped down from his horse and strode into the livery stable. The posse waited for Gulliver's order to dismount.

41

'Anyone here?' he shouted.

The horses shifted in their stalls but there was no answer.

'Boss, we ought to get the horses in the shade for a while,' Tucker suggested.

'Leave 'em here,' Gulliver snapped. 'We'll walk up to the saloon.'

Buck had his ear to the door in the back room of the saloon and heard the clatter of the posse's boots on the wooden floor.

'Know where that old timer from the livery stable has got to?' Gulliver demanded.

Charlie put down the glass he was polishing and leaned across the bar.

'Why would I know that?'

Gulliver bit his tongue.

'Want to feed and water the horses,' Gulliver said. 'If he ain't there we can't pay him.'

'Pay me,' Charlie said. 'Two bits for each horse.'

'You people,' Gulliver sneered. His hands closed into fists. 'What's to stop you taking the money and not telling him?'

'He's a working man same as me,' Charlie said. 'Wouldn't be right.'

Gulliver laughed.

'That big fella I asked you about earlier,' Gulliver said. 'He a working man too?'

Charlie shrugged. He picked up another glass and began polishing.

'That fella from the stable told us he lived north of here. Ain't nothing but salt flats and sagebrush to the north,' Gulliver said.

Charlie put down the glass and picked up another.

'Guess he made a mistake.'

'There's two of my men in his stable right now helping themselves to his hay and water. I don't feel inclined to leave my money with no saloon keeper. Guess I won't be able to pay him if he ain't there.'

Charlie continued working his way through the row of glasses.

'Any of your men plannin' on orderin' a drink?'

'We'll have six glasses of beer. What have you got to eat?'

'Mister.' Charlie placed the palms of his hands flat on the bar and leaned forward. 'This ain't no San Francisco chop house. We got whiskey but no beer, water but no ice. If you want to eat, you let me know a day in advance.'

Gulliver looked round at the swept floorboards, the repaired furniture and the cracked, oak-framed mirror on the wall.

'I'll take a whiskey,' Gulliver said. 'And give me a pitcher of water and five glasses.'

Buck slipped out through the back door and headed for the stable. Gulliver downed his whiskey and slapped some change on the bar. He strode to the window and stared out into the street. The light was failing. Shadows filled the spaces between the wooden buildings and the heat of the day slipped out of the air. While the men fell on the pitcher of water, Gulliver strolled back down to the stable. Buck was there remonstrating with the two men who had filled the trough from his pump and had helped themselves to his hay.

When Buck noticed him, Gulliver was leaning in the doorway.

'You sent us the wrong way, old fella.' Gulliver's words crept through his lips. 'Took my money for it.'

Gulliver fished a stogie out of his top pocket and patted the pockets of his jacket for matches. He turned to the two men.

'Horses drunk their fill?'

Buck watched him, a line of sweat forming across his forehead.

'I want to know where this big fella lives,' Gulliver said. 'Like I asked you before.'

The men led the horses outside. Gulliver found his matches and lit his cigar. Blue smoke wreathed around him. He dropped the match at his feet. Flames curled through the wisps of straw scattered across the dirt floor. Gulliver drew his .45 and pointed it at Buck's chest.

'South,' Buck said quickly. 'I said north. I meant south.'

Gulliver stepped aside from the flames.

'You owe me a dollar,' Gulliver said.

The flames ran across the floor toward the hay bales.

'Spent it,' Buck said. 'Dollar don't last long round here.'

Gulliver ignored him and strode out into the street to where the men were holding the horses. He holstered his gun and nodded to the men to mount up. Inside the stable, Buck snatched a bucket, dropped it in the trough and splashed water over the floor.

'South,' Gulliver said.

Outside town, the moonlit desert was full of shapes and the air was cold. Beaver tail cacti cast flat shadows, the cotton tops caught the moonlight like torn pillows and the petals of the snakeweed flowers were closed as tight as fists. A coyote howled somewhere. The riders bypassed a stand of mesquites which hung over a pool and continued on into the blackness.

'Boss,' Tucker said.

44

'No.' Gulliver turned towards him. 'We get there tonight.'

When they came to a house close to the dusty track, the door swung open at the first push. A shaft of moonlight fell on a bare wooden table and empty chairs. No people, no possessions, no livestock. The bark on one of the lower branches of the fig tree out front was rubbed bare where an animal had been tethered.

'How do you know this is the place, boss?' Tucker said.

Round the side of the house, Gulliver inspected the fire pit: the embers were still warm.

'Because it's empty,' Gulliver said.

'Three day ride to the border,' Tucker said.

'They shoot Gringos down there,' Gulliver said. 'Everyone knows that. Big guy like that, they'd go after him for sport.'

There was a shout from one of the men.

'Boss, there's tracks.'

Gulliver dismounted and strode over to where one of the men was kneeling on the ground.

'Two sets. One runs south, one runs north-east. The one that heads south is a mule.'

The man pointed to dark hoof prints in the silver sand.

'Edges is sharp,' the man continued. 'Sand ain't blowed over 'em yet.'

'Angel Pass is due south,' Tucker said.

'Think he'd head down there carryin' that payroll?' Gulliver said. 'I reckon he's doubled back.'

'Then who's headed south?' Tucker said.

'Didn't he have a Mexican woman?' Gulliver said. 'Could have sent her home.'

The sharp silver light dimmed as threads of cloud crossed the moon.

45

'Can't follow him now,' the tracker said.

A breeze touched the faces of the men.

'We'll get back to that pool and make a fire,' Gulliver said. 'Plenty of time to catch him in the morning.'

Lucas squeezed into a cleft in the rock and pulled his blanket round him. Even though he was sheltered by the cliff face, he dared not make a fire and the cold air cut him to the bone. Above him, clouds moved over the moon, covered and uncovered the banner of stars. He unwrapped the cloth which held the bread and tomatoes. The fruit was crisp and sour and the bread tasted of home.

Maria would be eating the same food, he thought. Her way was lit by the same moon and she looked up at the same stars. Lucas closed his eyes and imagined her riding over the cold land. He had pictures in his head of the way she glanced at the child whatever she was doing so he was always under her protective gaze.

Clouds quickened across the sky and filled the land with restless shadows. The night breeze lifted traces of sand from the desert floor. A family of cottontails scuttled from out between the rocks near his feet to feed on a clump of rice grass. The long, high bark of a coyote sounded far out in the desert. The rabbits froze for a second, stared at Lucas and returned to their meal.

# 5

Plataville was the end of the line. The great iron horse rested at the buffers while the driver fired up the boiler. Even though it was still dark, an armed man patrolled the rails and kept a lookout for the first shipment of the day. Lanterns hung along the side of the engine and the air smelled of smoke and oil. The sound of voices came from a wooden shack beside the lines where the rail-head guards kept out of the cold.

A mile away, Lucas headed up the pass which snaked from the desert floor to the plateau where the smelting works was sited next to the mine-shaft. The track was wide enough for two wagons and when dawn broke it would be in clear view of the rail-head from below and the smelting works from above. At one point in its climb, the track hair-pinned and narrowed between two walls of rock and for a few moments any rider would be out of sight. The dry bed of what had once been a stream cut down through the rock at the hairpin and clumps of onion grass and a yucca tree had found fissures in which to take root. There were two horses tied to the yucca, saddled, unattended and invisible from the works and the rail-head. On the plateau, an iron banner arched over a gateway: Plataville Silver

Mines, property of John Gulliver.

A line of fire burned along the horizon to the east. Lucas dismounted and led his horse under the sign. A collection of wooden buildings, sheds, stores, an office and a bunkhouse stood round a yard close to the entrance to the shaft. Further away, the doors to the smelting works were open. The place was lit by rows of oil lamps which hung from the ceiling. The red flames of the furnaces were visible and the bang and clang of hammers and the shouts of the men echoed inside. A wagon stood by one of the buildings already loaded with two wooden cases, straw sticking out where the lids were nailed down.

As Lucas watched, a man strutted out of the smelting works with short angry steps and climbed up on to the driver's seat. Gulliver junior ran after him.

'There ain't no places on the smelter this shift,' the man snapped. 'I can't figure why you don't want me to drive the cart same as I always do.'

His face flushed with anger, the man picked up the reins. Gulliver's hand rested on the side of the wagon.

'I got a new guy,' Gulliver said. 'I told you.'

'Yeah. Well you didn't tell the foreman to make a place for me on the shift. Why should I wait around for ten hours before I start work?'

A group of men watched from the doorway to the smelting works.

'Every time your pa is away, the place don't run right,' the man snapped. 'I've been with him since the beginning. He wouldn't want you taking me off the wagon for no reason.'

The man noticed Lucas.

'You the new guy?'

48

Lucas nodded. He rested his axe on the ground.

'Well, I'm sorry. But it ain't right.'

'Come on now,' Gulliver pleaded. 'You can have the day off.'

The man turned on Gulliver.

'What am I gonna do, play solitaire in the bunkhouse while the day shift is working and the night shift is asleep and not get paid for it?'

Men's faces were crowded at the window of the bunkhouse.

Gulliver smiled one of his big smiles.

'Take him with you,' Gulliver said. 'Show him what you do.'

'What for?' the man said. 'Don't he know how to drive a wagon?'

'He can ride along, can't he?' Gulliver said.

'When your pa gets back he won't want me off the wagon. I'm telling you that for free.'

The man turned to Lucas.

'OK fella, if you ain't got nothing else to do,' he said. 'What did you bring that axe for anyway?'

Lucas climbed up beside him.

'Belonged to my pa. He earned his living with it, same as me.'

Light flooded the sky. The red sun lifted above the horizon and the night chill promised to quit the air. The driver flicked the reins and the horses strained in their traces as the wagon creaked and moved forward. The group of men went back into the smelting works and suddenly there was no one at the window of the bunkhouse. Gulliver caught Lucas's eye but said nothing.

As the wagon pulled out of the yard, the driver turned to Lucas.

'Don't take no notice of that. Boss's son gets too big for his britches every time his pa is away. Name's Joe McCall.'

Lucas nodded.

'You gotta stand up for your rights even if you ain't got none,' McCall went on, letting his anger talk itself out.

'His pa ain't a bad boss if you keep on the right side of him. But this one. . . .' McCall chuckled to himself.

The wagon jolted over the rough track.

As they passed under the iron sign, McCall said 'I put that up a few years back. Had a Mexican blacksmith working here then. He made it and I put it up. Sure looked nice when it was new. Reckon the boss will want me to paint it again soon.'

'Been working here a long time?'

McCall laughed.

'Dug the first mine with John junior's pa. Reckon I worked just as many hours down in the ground as he did. Difference is, he owns all this while I ain't got nothing to show for it.'

'How come?' Lucas said.

McCall looked at him.

'Started out as partners till one night he took away my share in a poker game. He was cheatin' too, but I could never prove nothin'.'

'You stayed with him after that?'

McCall shrugged.

'Thought I'd win it back or roll up enough to stake my own claim.'

The wagon lurched on the stony track. McCall flicked the reins to encourage the horses.

'Never worked out that way. He bought the claims, I did the diggin'. That's the way it's been. John Gulliver ain't one to give a guy a second chance.'

The wagon started down the track towards the hairpin. Lucas glanced behind them. The yard was empty. Back inside the smelting shed there was the sound of hammering and men calling out to each other as they worked. The rock walls reared on either side of the wagon where the track narrowed. As they negotiated the hairpin, the two horses waited patiently beside the road.

'Hold up a minute,' Lucas said. 'Let me look at those horses.'

McCall turned to him.

'Just stop.'

Lucas felt the gun in his belt. McCall hauled on the reins.

'What for?'

Lucas jumped down from the wagon and unhitched one of the horses. He pulled open the saddle-bag and led it towards the wagon. Then he wrenched open one of the crates. Silver ingots nestled in straw like sleeping rabbits.

'Hey, what do you think you're doing?'

Lucas ignored McCall and lifted the ingots one by one into the saddle-bags.

'Hey. Damnit.'

Lucas looked at him.

'Don't try to stop me, mister. If you want, you can come with me. I'll cut you in.'

McCall reached under the seat and pulled out a shotgun.

'I mean it,' Lucas said. 'Half my share.'

'What are you sayin'?'

The shotgun wavered in McCall's hands.

'What d'you mean, half your share?'

'Other half belongs to John Gulliver junior.'

51

'You're crazy,' McCall said. 'It's his silver. Belongs to his family.'

'I ain't tellin' you what to do,' Lucas said. 'I'm makin' you an offer. If you refuse, I'm gonna take that gun off you and tie you up. But if you want, you can have a half share with me. You better make your mind up quick.'

Lucas started lifting the ingots into the second set of saddle-bags. McCall watched him, amazed.

'I could shoot you right now,' McCall said.

'You could.'

Lucas carried on working.

'I'm having to take that chance because I don't want to hurt you.'

'I ain't no thief,' McCall said.

'I'm a cutter,' Lucas said. 'From up at the charcoal camp. There was an accident and they're trying to say I murdered a man. I ran off. I lost my last month's pay and I won't be getting none this month. I got a wife and child. They're looking for me now and they ain't gonna stop till they find me. That's why I got to move fast.'

McCall lowered the shotgun.

'If some rich fella wants to pay me to take his own money, I reckon that's down to him,' Lucas went on. 'What he does with it ain't my concern.'

McCall put down the shotgun.

'You might count it as the boss stealing his own money,' he reflected. 'Don't reckon nobody else will.'

Lucas laced up the saddle-bags and tied his axe to the saddle.

'Can't take no more or the horses won't make it up that gully.'

'I worked all my life,' McCall said. 'What have I got to show for it? Half a bottle of Red Eye back in the

52

bunkhouse, a pack of cards and a bunch of IOU's I got to pay out come payday.'

'Want me to tie you up or slug you on the jaw?' Lucas said.

'Where are you headed?'

'Some place east. An old cantina out in the desert.'

'That would be Red Tail,' McCall said. 'You won't find it on your own. You'll give me a half share if I show you where it is?'

Lucas nodded.

'Chance like this don't come along more than once in a lifetime,' McCall said. 'High time it came to me.'

McCall climbed down from the wagon, looped the reins round the yucca tree and found stones to jam under the wheels.

'Be an hour or two before they send someone out looking for us.'

Both men mounted up. A careful horse could pick its way up the bed of the old stream and climb up on to the roof of the plateau. Stones rattled down the gully under the hoofs of their horses. The men pushed aside thorn bushes and fan palms which had taken root. Clumps of larkspur and desert lily decorated crevices in the rock walls. They leaned forward and whispered encouragement into the ears of their animals.

Where the gully became too steep, Lucas and McCall dismounted and led the horses. The bright morning sun was at their backs. A group of grey and brown pebbles turned into a family of collared lizards which broke cover and darted away among the stones as they approached. The gradient, the loose stones underfoot and the gathering heat of the day made the men catch their breath. As they reached the top, they could hear the noise of the smelting works again. They mounted up and took one last look back.

Down on the plain, the engine had built up a head of steam and a column of dark smoke reared into the morning sky. The rail-head looked empty, the men were all in the shade round the side of the wooden shack and across the gully, there was no one in the yard. Lucas and Joe McCall turned their horses east. The plateau was littered with untidy clutches of creosote bushes, the purple shapes of High Sierra rose far away to the north.

'Morning's ride,' McCall said. 'You got a gun?'

Lucas felt the pistol still shoved in his belt.

'Why?'

'Can't tell who you're going to meet there, that's all.'

McCall urged his horse into a gallop and Lucas followed.

When they stopped to rest the horses, McCall nodded towards the mountains on the horizon.

'Came out here when I was a kid. My pa reckoned he was gonna strike it rich. They all did back then.'

Lucas nodded.

'What happened?'

'Worked himself to death. My ma had got fed up with living in a tent and cooking in a Dutch oven years before that. Took off back to Missouri where she come from. I met up with Gulliver and worked with him when he bought his first silver claim. Gold was all dug out by then. Been with him ever since.'

McCall shrugged. 'Ain't much is it?'

'Got a wife?' Lucas said.

'Did have,' McCall said. 'What kind of life could I give her? Never had a big enough stake to get our own place. She dragged around after me for a few years, mining camp to mining camp. Gulliver was always going to make me foreman on the next claim, always going to give me a big raise next time there was a strike. Somehow company expenses swallowed up the profits and he never could afford it.' He smiled grimly. 'One day you look around and your whole life has just slipped away.'

McCall urged his horse forward and called over his shoulder to Lucas.

'Started living in the camp like the other guys, with a bottle of Red Eye and a pack of cards for company.'

A few trails of white cirrus clung to the empty sky.

'What about you?' McCall said. 'Always worked for Gulliver?'

'Got a farm,' Lucas said. 'Just a small place three days ride from the border. My wife's father built the house.'

'Lucky,' McCall said.

'Can't make a living on it,' Lucas said. 'Ground's rock hard all summer and floods every spring. That's why I signed on for wood cutting when they built the kilns.'

'What will you do with the money?' McCall said.

'Head for my wife's village across the border. People are poor down there, they need someone to set up a clinic. After that, buy a breeding mare and build up a farm. Guess I want something I can pass on to my son.'

'I'll go back East,' McCall said. 'Missouri. Buy a place back there.'

'Good farming country,' Lucas said.

'A place near a river,' McCall said. 'Willow trees hanging over it. I could take a fishing pole down there on the days when I wasn't working. Somewhere cool, where you could feel a breeze on your face.'

The men rode on over the barren ground and imagined how good their lives would be.

A wooden building constructed on stilts to compensate for the uneven ground was built into the side of a low cliff. The pitched roof was hidden behind a square façade which gave the structure a look of solidity it did not possess. A porch shaded by a ragged canvass awning ran along the front and a faded sign over the door read Red Tail Saloon. Beside the building was the disused entrance to an old mine-shaft, blocked with broken timbers buried in the rubble where the roof had caved in. Close by were the ruins of other buildings from what had been a mining settlement until the seams ran out and the bank fore-closed. A typical Mojave ghost town. A speckled rattler uncoiled itself from one of the stilts and slithered away under the saloon as Lucas and Joe dismounted.

'Stay here,' Lucas said and handed Joe the reins to his horse.

Lucas climbed the wooden steps and pushed open the saloon door. As his eyes were used to the bright sunlight outside, a wall of darkness faced him. The door swung closed. Waiting for his vision to adjust to the shadows, he heard a metallic snick as the hammer of a Colt was drawn back. Then he felt the cold barrel pressed against the side of his neck. Someone pulled the six-gun out of his belt and shoved him, still blinded by the darkness, further into the room.

**6**

The heat of the day was rising and the pace of the burro was wearyingly slow. Maria dismounted when she came to a stand of cottonwoods. She sat in the shade and held the child to her breast. Sunlight played through the square leaves and a breeze gave some relief from the burning sun. She could stay here for a few hours until the heat of the day passed.

In the distance, riders kicked up a dust cloud. Maria noticed them earlier crossing back and forth, circling round as if they were lost. Or searching for someone. These must be the men Lucas had spoken about. They had come from the direction of the house, maybe they had found out where he lived.

The child fed with contented concentration while sunlight dappled over him through the shifting leaves. Once Maria started to look into his face, she never wanted to look away. She could stare at him forever, the tiny movement of his mouth, his eyelids, every small shift in the muscles of his cheeks. She stroked his black curls with the back of her finger.

Without opening his eyes, the baby pulled away from her. A trace of milk was at the corners of his mouth. He

57

gave a cough, just to clear his throat. It was the smallest sound but her gaze intensified for a moment in case there should be something wrong. The child slipped from contented feeding into blissful sleep.

Having unhitched the basket from the saddle, Maria laid the child down in the shade. She adjusted the cotton sheet around his tiny body, careful in case he was too hot or too cool or the sheet was tight or loose. But the child slept on unconcerned. The leaves rustled above them. The burro found a patch of couch grass. She tore her eyes away from the sleeping child and leaned back against the trunk of the cottonwood.

The buzz of cicadas filled Maria's ears and the sun warmed her face. She took a mouthful of water from her cantina and unwrapped the square of cotton cloth which held bread and tomatoes. The fruit was too sharp for her taste, she never ate tomatoes this early in the year but Lucas loved them like this even more than when they had ripened. She should have given him more. He could have had hers.

Maria realized with a jolt that the drumming hoof beats were closer, the riders were heading in her direction. A cloud of brown dust followed them in the air. Had they seen her? She gathered the child out of the basket with one arm and grabbed the shotgun from where it was tucked under the saddle. She sat down against the tree. Then stood up. She did not know what to do. She sat down again and cradled the child close. The baby woke and started a soft mewling cry like a kitten. She stood up again and rocked the child back and forth. She did not want to put the shotgun down, but she couldn't fire it with one hand. She leant it against the tree and concentrated on rocking the child. The riders were close now, their hoofbeats rang against the desert floor.

The riders reined in their horses hard. Tired, angry faces, six of them. The one in charge leaned forward in his saddle and called down to her.

'Lookin' for someone,' he said. 'Someone who works for me.'

Maria held the baby close. He struggled in her arms. Was she holding him too tight? His cries were short and insistent.

'John Gulliver,' the man said. 'Fella I'm looking for works up at the charcoal camp.'

Maria watched the way his mouth was smiling. Lank grey hair fell from under his hat.

'He's a cutter up there,' Gulliver continued. 'There was an accident. I reckon old Lucas thinks he's killed a man and is gonna get the blame for it, but he ain't.'

When she heard Lucas's name it shocked her. Did it show on her face? Did John Gulliver know who she was?

'Reckon he got scared and just took off.'

Gulliver laughed and looked round at his men.

'I can understand that. Fella thinks no one ain't gonna believe him.'

Gulliver lowered his voice and spoke softly and reasonably.

'Matter of fact, I'm holding the wages I owe him. Can't pay him if I don't know where he is.'

He looked round at the riders again. See how reasonable I am. Look how well I treat my men. They were all grinning at him, agreeing. Maria looked into the faces of the men. Masks. Smiling masks which agreed with the boss whatever he said. She rocked the baby but his cries were louder now.

'I'm gonna ask you a question.'

Gulliver's smile fell from his face.

'Ain't no cause to be afraid. Just answer me straight.'

Maria stared at him. The child twisted in her arms.

'I ain't afraid of you mister.'

'Fella I'm looking for, Lucas Redwood. You wouldn't happen to be his woman would you?'

'I'm his wife,' Maria said.

'Wife?' Gulliver echoed. His eyes narrowed.

The child's cries broke into a yell of frustrated rage.

'Mind telling me where he's at?' Gulliver said.

'He don't tell me where he goes,' Maria said.

'If I knew where he was, I could let you have his pay right now because I'd know he was coming back for it.' Gulliver's words were oil.

'Let me talk to her, boss,' Tucker said. 'I got a way with Mexican women.'

The men laughed. When Maria looked at Tucker, she saw that the grin which slid round his mouth was not a mask at all. This was who he was, insolent and cruel.

'I told you. I don't know where he is,' Maria said.

Gulliver's eyes hardened.

'Boss,' Tucker said. 'I could—'

Gulliver ignored him.

'And where are you going?'

'That ain't your business,' Maria said.

The child screamed. She rocked it back and forth but it made no difference.

'Looks to me like you're headed south,' Gulliver said. 'Most likely headed for the border. Closest crossing to here is Angel Pass. Take you two days on that mule.'

'Boss, let me—'

'Shut up, Tucker.'

Gulliver turned back to Maria. His eyes bored into her.

'Reckon your husband intends to meet you at the border,' Gulliver said. 'If we don't pick him up first.'

Maria tried to comfort the child. Rage mottled his face.

Gulliver yanked on the reins of his horse.

'Ain't we gonna take her with us, boss?' Tucker said. 'She could ride up behind me.'

'She'd slow us down,' Gulliver said. 'We know where she's headed.'

The men wheeled their horses.

'We got to find this fella,' Gulliver said. 'I'm getting sick of riding round in circles. Sure don't want to ride all the way down to the border unless I have to.'

The men dug in their spurs and the horses leapt forward in a spray of dust.

Maria looked into the face of the child. His eyes were open. He stopped crying and lay still, watching her. Bubbles of joy rested at the corners of his lips. She sat down and leaned back against the trunk of the cotton-wood and looked out over the desert. The riders disappeared under a cloud of dust, the drum of their horses' hoofs slowly faded. They were riding into the heat of the day. Where the pale sky met the flat land, pools and eddies shimmered in the air like knots in glass.

For the first time, Maria feared for Lucas. Gulliver was used to getting his own way, he would not give up. And he was sharp. How had he worked out that she and Lucas planned to meet at the border? Maybe she should get going now, ride through the heat. But what difference would it make. Gulliver knew where she was and where she was headed. She looked down at the child. He was sleep-ing again. She placed him in the basket, lay down beside him with her head on the crook of her arm and listened to his infant snores.

*

Explosions of steam punched the air, the great pistons thrust into life and the wheels inched round. As the engine shunted back the line of trucks, couplings clanged together and the driver leaned out of his cab. Some way out across the plain two riders reined in their horses and turned to look.

'What's that driver doing? He said he would wait?'

This was William Schott the head security guard, a tall tough looking man with a pair of Colts in his gun-belt and two Winchesters in saddle-holsters. His companion was Carl Fuddle, shorter, round faced, a single Colt at his hip.

'Boss is away,' Fuddle said. 'Everything's gone to hell. Always does.'

'That driver,' Schott said. 'He told me.'

'Could catch him,' Fuddle suggested. 'One of us could ride back.'

'I got to think,' Schott said. 'Boss is gonna crawl across the sky when he hears about this.'

Fuddle fell silent.

'You were supposed to be on look out,' Schott added.

Fuddle didn't answer.

'What am I going to tell Gulliver?' Schott said.

Fuddle looked straight ahead of him over the plain to the dirt track which climbed up on to the plateau.

'I was watching out for the wagon,' Fuddle said.

'You were supposed to watch the time as well.'

'Maybe Joe McCall's sick,' Fuddle said. 'Maybe that's why the wagon ain't come.'

'Joe?' Schott said. 'Ain't never had a day off work in his life. Takes a pride in it.'

The sun was climbing the sky now. The men were glad

to be riding towards the pass where there was some shade. At first it was a shallow climb.

'There it is,' Fuddle shouted.

The wagon was tucked in the corner of the hairpin with stones under the wheels and the horses reins looped around a yucca. Schott leapt down from his saddle.

'Crates is busted open. Look at that.'

The men were amazed.

'How come you never saw this?' Schott said. 'You must have seen the wagon leave and get this far?'

'Where's Joe?' Fuddle said.

He started to look round wildly.

'You don't think . . .'

Schott unholstered a pistol.

'How come you didn't see 'em?'

'They must have gone back up to the smelter,' Fuddle said. 'They never came down at all.'

Fuddle had his gun in his hand now. Sweat soaked the back of his shirt. He expected someone to jump out at him at any second so he tried to look everywhere.

'I'll ride back down and get the guys,' Schott said.

'No.' Fuddle yelped. 'I ain't staying here on my own. They ain't took half of what's in the crates. What if they come back?'

His eyes danced over the rocks. If there was a gang and it came back, Schott thought, he would lose all the silver and Gulliver would hold him responsible.

'Smelter's nearer than the rail-head,' he said. 'We'll turn her around.'

'Wish I knew what they've done with Joe McCall,' Fuddle said.

Schott kicked the stones away from under the wagon wheels and unlaced the reins from the yucca.

'You drive.'

He handed the reins to Fuddle and climbed back on his horse.

'Reckon they went up there?' Fuddle said.

He indicated the narrow gully where the stream had once run.

'Sprung out of the wagon right here, took the silver and headed up the cliff.'

Schott shaded his eyes and examined the climb.

'Too steep,' Schott said. 'I wouldn't ride up there.'

Fuddle climbed up on to the wagon and negotiated a turn in the road.

'Wish I knew what had happened to Joe.'

There was no one about when the wagon pulled under the iron sign into the yard. The usual sound of machinery rang from the open smelting shop door. The shouts and laughter of the men echoed from inside.

'This ain't gonna be easy,' Schott said. His naturally worried looking face was drained. He dismounted and walked over to the wooden shack with the manager's sign on the door. Fuddle saw him hesitate before he went in.

In a second, he was back in the yard again.

'No one there,' he called to Fuddle.

Schott went into the smelting shop. Minutes later, the sound of machinery and the voices of the men died. He emerged with a group of men who set about examining the wagon and the broken packing cases. One of the men banged on the bunkhouse door where the second shift guys were sleeping.

'You got Joe McCall in there?'

'Where's the boss?' Schott said.

'Over at the charcoal camp,' one of the men said. 'Left John junior in charge. Ain't seen him all morning.'

'Anyone know where John junior is?' Schott appealed to the others. They all shook their heads.

'We got to get this down to the rail-head, where I got men to guard it.'

'I ain't driving it down,' Fuddle said. 'Not on my own. Not without a proper guard. This ain't my silver and I'm gonna get canned anyway because of this.'

A man emerged from the bunkhouse and blinked in the sunlight.

'Joe drove the wagon down at first light. Ain't come back yet.'

He stared at the wagon.

'What's happened?'

'Come on,' Schott said. 'I got a rifle. You guys hear any shooting you come runnin'.'

He mounted up, rode beside the wagon.

'What about Joe?' Fuddle said.

'Never mind him,' Schott said. 'We got to get this down and under guard before something else happens.'

Fuddle flicked the reins and called out to the horses. The men watched the wagon leave.

'You stay close with that rifle,' Fuddle called. 'I ain't taking a bullet for someone else's silver.'

# 7

'Nobody knows you and nobody suspects me, remember?'
Gulliver junior's voice was taut with anger.

Lucas blinked in the darkness. The old saloon smelled
of dust and sweat. The cold barrel of a Colt dug into his
neck.

'Who else did you tell about this?'

As Lucas's eyes adjusted, shapes rose out of the darkness – chairs, tables. He felt the gun barrel pull away from
his neck. In the mirror behind the bar, Lucas saw Gulliver
junior step away from him, his Colt still leveled at Lucas's
back.

'Sit down.'

Gulliver kicked a chair to show him.

Gulliver took a chair across the table from Lucas and
kept his gun pointed at him.

'Should have got rid of McCall,' Gulliver said. 'Did you
get the silver?'

'All we could carry.'

Grey light filtered through a window caked in sand and
dirt. Lines of sunlight drew round the edges of the door
and slashed the walls where the cottonwood planks had
warped. Gulliver holstered his gun and stuffed Lucas's

into his belt.

'Could have carried it all if you'd come by yourself,' he snapped.

'I've told him,' Lucas said. 'He can have half my share.'

'That ain't it,' Gulliver said. 'Soon as they catch up with him, he'll tell 'em I was here.'

Gulliver pushed his chair back, got to his feet and started to pace. His boot heels clacked on the wooden floor.

'Should have got rid of him.'

'Just give him his money,' Lucas said. 'He'll hightail it. He don't want to stay around here.'

Gulliver's heels hammered into the floor.

'Money ain't here yet,' he snapped.

The door swung open. Joe McCall's silhouette stood against the sunlight. Gulliver went for his gun and covered the doorway. Joe peered into the darkness.

'Anyone there?'

'All right Joe,' Lucas said. 'Just wait outside.'

'Getting kind of edgy,' Joe said. 'On my own out here.'

'Just wait outside.'

McCall turned and the door swung shut.

'See?' Gulliver hissed. 'Why didn't you get rid of him?'

Gulliver crossed to the window and stared out across the plain. Joe McCall sat on the porch with his back to the door and rolled a cigarette. Gulliver took precise aim and pointed his gun at the back of McCall's head. He pretended to fire, making the sound of a shot with his lips, then blew the imaginary smoke away from the barrel of the gun.

'When's the guy with the money gonna be here?' Lucas said.

'Anyone follow you?' Gulliver said. 'Guys from the rail-head?'

'Didn't see no one,' Lucas said. 'Probably found the wagon by now.'

'Got to get rid of McCall,' Gulliver said.

He flung open the door and stepped on to the porch. McCall dropped his cigarette and jumped up. Lucas ran outside after Gulliver.

'Joe,' Gulliver said.

McCall pulled at the brim of his hat.

'Boss.'

'Got a proposition for you,' Gulliver said.

McCall's eyes darted between Gulliver and Lucas.

'You know that this silver is mine.'

McCall nodded.

'Means that so far you ain't done nothing wrong.'

McCall stared at him.

'You worked for my pa for a long time, Joe. I'm gonna give you one of these bars of silver. You can ride away right now. Nobody can blame you for nothing.'

McCall looked to Lucas.

'You said a half share.'

'Money ain't here, Joe,' Lucas said. 'He's offering you a way out.'

'When's the money coming?' McCall said. 'How long have we got to wait?'

'They'll be starting after you right now,' Gulliver said. 'Most likely started already. They won't talk to you nice like I am. They'll shoot you down first time they see you.'

'I dunno,' McCall said.

Worry lined his face, his mouth set tight. He searched the horizon for a dust cloud which would mean they had been followed. A rattler coiled itself round one of the supports under the building to bask in the heat. McCall shook his head, unable to decide what to do.

'What about you, Lucas?'

'He's stayin',' Gulliver snapped.

'I never had nothin',' McCall said. 'My whole life is just working, dragging round from mine to mine, waiting on the next payday, waiting on the next job. Been doing this for years and what have I got? All found in a bunkhouse and a bunch of IOU's.'

'What are you talking about?' Gulliver said.

'I'm talking about me,' McCall said. 'My life. That's what I'm talking about.'

He turned to Lucas.

'You said a half share. That's what I want so I can go to Missouri and buy a place.'

Gulliver's gun was in his hand.

'You're making a mistake Joe. I'm giving you a chance.'

'You're the boss's son, you don't understand nothing. One bar of silver ain't enough for a lifetime.'

Gulliver fixed McCall with his cold eyes and pulled back the hammer of his Colt.

An avalanche of dirt and stones scattered down the cliff face and thundered over the roof of the saloon. McCall and the others leapt down off the porch. More stones clattered over the shingles and kicked up dust where they hit the ground. The men ran out from the building and stared up at the cliff face. A man stood amongst a tangle of creosote bushes, his Winchester was at his shoulder trained on them.

'Put that gun aside,' the man called. 'Don't want no accidents.'

Gulliver shoved his Colt back in its holster.

'On the dirt, in front of you,' the man said. 'And the one in your belt.'

Gulliver threw the guns down in front of him.

'You other fella's packin'?'

The man kicked some more loose rocks down on to the saloon roof. The horses tied to the rail outside the saloon stamped and twisted at their reins.

'Anyone else inside?'

'No one else here,' Gulliver said.

A second man appeared from behind the first and began to scramble down the cliff face. The roots of the creosote bush, stones and dried mud gave away under him and he ended up sliding vertically down the dusty wall. At the bottom he picked up his hat and dusted himself down. As soon as he took a Colt out of his holster to cover Gulliver and the others, the first man leapt down on to the roof and then sprang on to the ground.

The two men covered them – one with a Colt, the other with his Winchester. The men were both young with scraps of beards on their cheeks. The one with the Winchester was tall and quick. His shirt was faded and his jeans were torn at the knees. The one who had slid down the cliff was heavier built and the exertion had made him short of breath. Cruelty mixed with mockery in their eyes.

'What have we got here?' the one with the Winchester said.

The young men looked them up and down.

'Well?' he went on.

He jerked the Winchester towards Lucas.

'You first big fella.'

'They don't know nothin',' Gulliver said. 'I'm the one in charge. John Gulliver.'

Gulliver paused expecting them to recognize his name.

'From the silver mine,' he added.

The man holding the Winchester looked at him.

'No you ain't. I know what he looks like and you ain't

70

him. You ain't old enough for a start.'

There was a metallic snick as the second man pulled back the hammer of his Colt.

'That's my pa you're talking about,' Gulliver said. 'I'm John Gulliver junior.'

'Well, John Gulliver junior from the silver mine, you can just wait your turn because I'm talking to the big fella.'

'Come out here to meet somebody,' Lucas said. 'Waiting for 'em right now.'

'What about you, old timer?' He waved his Winchester in McCall's direction.

'I'm just a workin' man. Drive a wagon for the mining company.'

He turned back to Gulliver.

'And you're the boss of this outfit?'

A grin slipped across Gulliver's mouth.

'We ain't come here to bother you, friend,' Gulliver said.

The man stared at him hard. He spat a stream of tobacco saliva into the dust.

'Reckon I should shoot 'em all now, Curly, or wait till Emmet gets here?'

'Now just a minute,' McCall blustered. 'I ain't done nothin'. You ain't got no quarrel with me.'

'Shoot 'em,' Curley said.

'Mister,' Gulliver said. 'Please.'

'See,' the man stepped forward and prodded Gulliver in the chest with his rifle. 'We know what's in your saddle-bags.'

Curly laughed.

'We know why you come out here and who you're waiting for.'

The smile disappeared from Gulliver's mouth.

71

'Mister,' McCall pleaded.

'Shut up, working man. You ain't no working man now. You crossed the line when you came out here. You're one of us now.'

McCall whimpered.

'Emmet Jackson,' Gulliver persisted. 'He's the fella I'm waiting for. You know him?'

His grin slung round his mouth again.

'I'm Leonard Jackson and this here is Curly. Emmet is our pa. He's on his way out here right now. Sent us on ahead just in case you brought someone with you, seeing as he agreed to meet you on his own.'

'Had to have someone help haul the silver,' Gulliver said.

'Looks to me like you brought two fellas with you when you said you would be here alone. Looks to me like you was intending to ambush Pa and take the money.'

Leonard spat again. The men watched the pool of brown saliva settle in the dust.

'You just sit down on the porch and we'll wait for Pa. Make one move and we'll blow your heads off.'

'Look—' Gulliver began.

'Did I say speak?'

The men stared out across the plain. The sun was high now and the air moved in the heat. Curly covered them with his Colt while Leonard went off to inspect the saddle-bags. The speckled rattler unwound itself from the support under the building and slid past them.

'Ain't all here,' Leonard said as he unlaced the last saddle-bag.

'I can explain that,' Gulliver said.

Leonard glared at him.

'Looks like you was going to take Pa's money when you

ain't given him all the silver.'

Far out across the plain a dust cloud twisted in the hot air.

'Save your explainin',' Leonard said. 'Pa's comin'.'

Joe McCall tried again.

'Mister, just let me go now. I didn't ought to be here. I'll just ride away. I never saw nothing.'

Leonard let McCall's plea hang in the air and stared out across the flat land. The men's attention was focused on the pillow of brown dust which shifted in the heat. Suddenly Leonard cocked his Winchester.

'Ain't Pa,' he said.

'What?' Curley said.

'I'm telling you. There's more than one.'

Leonard rounded on Gulliver.

'You done this.'

Gulliver pushed himself back on the porch, his eyes on the barrel of the Winchester.

'You was going to take Pa's money. Now you brought a posse after you to get the silver back off Pa.'

He jabbed the Winchester in Gulliver's gut. Gulliver looked around wildly.

'I ain't got an idea who they are, no more than you.'

The riders were approaching fast now. Their hoof beats rang against the iron ground. Leonard waved the Winchester at Lucas.

'Get that silver inside,' he snapped. He gestured to McCall. 'And you help him.'

McCall and Lucas got to their feet just as the first shot cracked the air. One man was out in front of the riders, his Colt in his hand, firing as his horse pounded forward. Lucas slung the bags inside the saloon and ran to help McCall. Leonard shoved Gulliver through the door like a

73

sack. A second pistol shot sang through the air and tore splinters off the edge of the wooden wall. Gulliver was shouting to be allowed to get his guns. Curly flung himself through the door. Lucas pushed Joe McCall inside and threw a second pair of saddle-bags after him. A third shot cracked, but the bullet whined and went wide.

Leonard crouched by the window and smashed a corner pane with his Winchester. At the first rifle shot, the riders wheeled away back out of range. Lucas hurled himself in through the open door and snatched up the Colts Gulliver had thrown in the dirt. Leonard turned the Winchester on him.

'I'll take those.'

Lucas ignored him and tossed one of the Colts to Gulliver.

'Those guys out there want us dead,' Lucas said. 'Shooting each other is only going to do their job for 'em.'

Leonard's finger tightened on the trigger. Lucas faced him without flinching.

'They've split up.' Curley was at the window.

After a second, Leonard lowered the Winchester.

'You're a brave man,' Leonard said.

'Can't tell where they're headed,' Curly called.

Gulliver slid up behind Leonard, pulled back the hammer of his Colt and shoved it in his back.

'I should blow you in half right now.'

'Don't be a fool,' Lucas said.

Curly had turned away from the window and covered Gulliver with his Colt.

Gulliver grinned and clicked the hammer shut.

'For now,' he said.

'They're circling round behind,' Joe McCall said. 'There's easy climbing up on to the ridge half a mile each side of here.'

Lucas shoved the pistol in his belt.

'Once they get up on that ridge, they got us nailed,' McCall said. 'Only thing we can do then is to ride back the way we come.'

'Towards the rail-head?'

'Any other direction you're riding into a great big nothing. If you ain't carrying water, you ain't got a prayer.'

The men stood in the doorway and watched the two groups of riders head off into the shimmering air. Above them a red tailed kite hovered for a moment and then used its wing tips to uplift on to the thermals and glide in graceful circles which stretched wide across the sky.

'How long d'you reckon we've got?' Leonard said.

'We head out for the rail-head, they'll be on us before we get there,' McCall said. 'We try to get the horses up the slope at the back of the saloon, they'll be here before we reach the top.'

'You know this place, old timer?'

'Ought to,' McCall said. 'Dug most of that shaft out there. One of his pa's first claims.'

He nodded towards Gulliver.

'Thought it was gonna be a big strike but the seam ran out within the year.'

'We got to stand and fight then?' Curley said. 'We don't even know who they are.'

'I do,' Gulliver said.

# 8

The cutting teams trudged back down the hillside as dusk fell. Exhausted after their work, the men were silent as the kidding which sustained them through the day was used up. They carried their saws and axes with them to be sharpened for the morning. Two of the kilns were lit and the smell of smoke tainted the air. The rows of tents were perched along the hillside like birds on a wire. Bill Wheeling stood on the office porch holding his knife, spoon and tin plate waiting for the first clang of the cook's triangle.

As Tucker and the boss had not yet returned, Wheeling was in charge. His posse had spent the day combing the woods and lower slopes while the men worked. If Lucas had been there, they would have found him. He was glad they hadn't. The bag containing the payroll was stuffed inside the blankets on his bunk where he and Tucker had left it. The office was the only place in the camp Gulliver hadn't thought to search.

The men filed past Wheeling as they headed for their tents. One or two acknowledged him with a nod but most ignored him. They could spare him a word of greeting as they walked past even though they were tired, couldn't they? Wheeling knew the men didn't like him. He told himself it was because he was foreman. What could you expect? They didn't like taking orders and were jealous. But there was something else. The men always took their problems to Tucker, never to him.

Wheeling knew the cutters were deliberately slow to react whenever he told them to do something and were resentful when he pointed out areas of the woods they should work in. Any time he made a suggestion to the charcoal burners, they ignored him altogether. This evening, unless he received a friendly word from the cook when he took his place first in line, he would eat alone at the foreman's table and no one would speak to him.

Still wearing the gun-belt he had had on all day, Wheeling hurried down towards the cook tent when the triangle sounded. Some of the men had already formed a line. He walked to the head of it and held out his plate. The cook called out instructions to his assistant, ladled his chops and beans and barely looked at him. Wheeling muttered a thanks but the cook was already dishing out the next man's food. As he headed for the foreman's table he felt the men in the queue watching him.

Cutters took their seats at the table next to Wheeling's. The man closest to him was someone he knew, Wheeling couldn't remember his name but he had seen him around the camp. Next to him was another man Wheeling knew. He couldn't remember his name either but recalled him because they had talked about fishing when the man first came to work there. He was a pleasant mannered guy, popular amongst the men.

Wheeling stood up, picked up his plate and crossed to the table where the men were sitting. There was one empty space.

'This anyone's?' Wheeling said. He forced a smile. 'Ain't no sense in sitting over there by myself.'

Immediately, he wished he hadn't said that. He wished he hadn't explained. It made it sound as though he was asking for a favour.

The man looked up. Wheeling wished he could remember his name.

'Anyone's?' Wheeling indicated the empty seat.

The man looked surprised.

'It's took.'

The man nodded at Wheeling's shoulder. Wheeling turned. The Mexican, Caborca, was standing behind him with his plate of food in his hand.

'I was just—' Wheeling said.

Wheeling stepped aside to let Caborca sit down.

Back at his own table, Wheeling stared down at his food and ate quickly. He didn't look up because he knew the men would be staring at him. Not staring, just glances now and then. Then he realized he was eating too fast. He would finish before everyone else and be sitting there with no one to talk to with an empty plate in front of him. When Tucker was there, they sat at the table after the meal, joked about the manager and smoked cigarettes for an hour sometimes while the cutters sharpened their axes for the morning. Wheeling put down his knife, stared into the distance as if some thought had crossed his mind and avoided catching the eye of any of the men.

The sound of conversation spread across the tables. It was always like this in the evenings. Everyone was silent at the start of the meal and didn't talk until they had got some food inside them. The cook called out for seconds. There was a rush of men to form a queue as there was never enough for everyone. Wheeling started eating again. He wouldn't be the first to finish now.

When Wheeling looked up, Caborca was standing in front of him.

'See any sign of Lucas today?'

The question startled Wheeling. He had been going over in his mind what he would say when Gulliver asked him the same thing. He would have to make it sound as though they had searched everywhere they thought of, even though they had missed some of the higher stretches above the tree line which would have meant abandoning their horses and climbing the steep ground on foot.

Wheeling shook his head. What did the Mexican want? Why was he asking him?

'You searched everywhere in the camp for the money?' Caborca went on.

The words rang in Wheeling's ears.

'You know we did.'

The men from the nearby table stopped talking.

'What's it to you anyway?'

'Me and the guys,' Caborca said. 'We don't reckon Lucas would have done this. We ain't saying we're better than anybody, but there ain't a single one of us would have took the payroll. We got wives and families. That's the money they live on. Now the boss is gonna say he can't pay us.'

Wheeling knew he could deal with this Mexican.

'Evidence is right there. Man's dead. Money's gone. Lucas has run off.'

He sat back and folded his arms. No one could argue with the facts.

'But nobody saw him,' Caborca persisted. 'And nobody reckons he's got it in him anyway. You know Lucas. You think he could have done it?'

Wheeling hesitated. The men from the other table were listening.

'Could have,' he said cautiously. 'He's a strong guy.'

Wheeling thought of something else.

'If Lucas didn't do it, who did?'

One by one the men from the other table got to their feet. Instead of making their way back towards the tents they came and stood beside Caborca. Wheeling felt a wave of panic rise inside him. Why couldn't he remember their names?

'You and Tucker been telling us the company ain't making enough profit,' one of the men said. 'That's why the boss was coming up.'

Wheeling looked from one to the other of them. They were all ranged against him.

'Good way of saving money is not to pay the guys,' the man went on. 'I've worked in lumber camps before.'

'You saw the payroll wagon arrive yesterday. Everyone did. It was locked in the safe as usual.'

Wheeling was being forced to defend Gulliver and his business. The man seemed to blame everything on him and Tucker, falling profits, the men's work rate, even the distance the camp was from the tree line. Couldn't they see he couldn't speak for the boss?

'The money went missing about the time the boss was here,' Caborca continued.

'One thing no one ain't considered is if the boss took it.' A short, muscular man spoke. Wheeling had seen him work; he handled an axe well.

Wheeling laughed. How could they be so stupid? It reminded him of why he was foreman and not them and gave him back confidence.

'You guys better get back and sharpen up them axes,'

Wheeling said. 'We got an early start.'

'Ain't you hearing what we're saying?' the man said.

Colour rose in Wheeling's neck. The man's question lit a flame of anger inside him.

'What's your name anyway?' Wheeling said.

The man stared at him.

'I've been working here ten months. Don't you know my name?'

He looked round at the others. No one spoke but Wheeling knew they were laughing at him. They disliked him, they were jealous of him, they refused to let him eat with them and now they were laughing at him.

'Henry Meadows,' the man said.

Wheeling stood up.

'What we're saying,' Caborca said, 'is that the boss could have took the money out of the safe.'

Other men had joined the group now.

'That's bull,' Wheeling said. 'He rode off with the posse. He didn't have no payroll with him. You saw him ride off.'

The men's eyes bored into him. Dislike, jealousy, laughter.

'Pablo's right,' Henry Meadows said. 'He could have took the payroll out of the safe and hid it before he rode out with the posse.'

'We searched,' Wheeling said. His own voice sounded thin and strained. Would the men think he was afraid of them? 'We searched the whole camp. All the tents.'

'Everywhere?'

'Everywhere except the company office,' Meadows said. 'Boss could have hid the payroll in there. He knows none of the men go in there. Only people who go in there is you and Tucker. You both been out riding all day. Boss could

81

be aiming to come back for it later.'

Wheeling knew what they were going to ask now. And he knew fear showed in his face. They would all see it and they would know he was frightened of them. They had tricked him. First dislike, then jealousy, then laughter and now they had made him into a fool.

'We want to search the office,' Meadows said. 'You and all of us together so that nobody can't be accused of nothing.'

Wheeling snatched his gun from its holster. Shock registered on the men's faces.

'I'm foreman,' Wheeling barked. 'Nobody searches the company office.'


Sleeping with the child in the crook of her arm, Maria knew the exact time when the note of his breathing changed. She had built a fire which gave a meagre halo of warmth in the lee of a spread of creosote bushes. She pulled a blanket round herself and the child as the temperature fell to freezing. Above her, stars glittered like ice crystals and the moon filled the landscape with cold monochrome light. A coyote yowled in the distance and another answered in the shadows close by.

Having made a bed as close to the fire as she dared, Maria stretched out gratefully, lay the shotgun beside her and made a place for the child. Sleep teased her, came close but never quite arrived. Her arm was numb where she held the child but she did not move for fear of waking him. Another day and another night and the next day she would be at the border. Lucas would be waiting and everything would be fine.

Some time later, Maria woke with a start. Pairs of yellow eyes watched her from the darkness on the other side of the fire. She moved quickly but before she could pick up a piece of wood to fling at them, the coyotes had scampered away. It was then she heard the child's breathing.

When they lay down, his breathing had been even and noiseless. Now there was wire in his throat, gasps scratched his palate and his chest buckled with every breath. Maria held him close to the firelight to see his face. His eyes were screwed tight with effort, his beautiful mouth was bent with pain. She loosened the cotton blankets to ease the pressure on his chest.

As Maria watched, the child's face broke and he started to cry. Tiny, rasping cries. A universe of torment. Maria touched his forehead with her cheek. His body was burning. She loosened the cloths further and rocked him gently in her arms but his tiny choking breaths and forlorn cries persisted and she did not know if she was making him better or worse. She stood up and walked round the fire. Maybe the motion of her steps would ease him. His sobs jerked as every breath caught in his throat.

Maria could feel the heat of his body through the cotton cloths now. She recalled herbal mixtures her mother had taught her. If she were at home, it would be easy. The herbs would be to hand or she would know where to find them. The child's crying flared as frustration amplified his pain.

Away to the east, the darkness weakened. Maria tried to put the child to her breast but he struggled away from her, turned his head and arched his back. His unending, choking cries drove into her like nails until she felt his pain with him. And he began to cough. His chest heaved and he writhed in her arms as he tried to shed the agony like a skin. The cough rattled each breath, strangled each helpless gasp of air. Maria cradled him in her arms close to her heart and stood staring at the lightening sky, she swayed back and forth from her hips – the motion she used at home to make him sleep – but his pain continued, pitiful cries tore his chest.

Maria willed him to stop. She stood there swaying him back and forth, willing him to be calm. She concentrated all her thoughts, all her love for him, to make him still and to make his pain disappear. She would gladly have taken it all on herself just to give him a moment's relief.

Nightmare thoughts filled Maria's head: his crying would never stop and he would never recover. She knew how frail life could be. Her mother had buried children, two of her sisters. When she was a child, a girl who she played with in the village suddenly took sick and died. The first sign that something was wrong was a cough.

Fear inhabited her. Maybe the child was dying. How could she tell? No one ever knew until the end when it was too late. There was never anything you could do. There were the herbal tinctures her mother had taught her that was all. All the children from the village who had died had been given those tinctures. The women had searched the ground for miles to find the right ingredients but the children had still died.

The child bucked back and forth in her arms, each breath choked by screams. How could his little body stand this for so long? If he just lay still he would feel better, breath would come more easily. She shushed him and blew little gusts of breath on his cheek to distract him. She tried to catch his attention with snatches of the old songs her mother had taught her.

As the beginnings of daylight pushed the darkness aside, the shapes which surrounded her returned, the creosote bushes, the ashes of the fire, the blanket she had lain on. She wrapped the child again more loosely than before. His jagged cries persisted as she tied the basket on to the saddle of the burro and mounted up. She tore off a handful of tortilla, bit into one of the green tomatoes and swigged water from her canteen.

If she could find a cottonwood, Maria would be able to boil pieces of its bark to make a tincture. She could squeeze a few drops on to the child's lips from a piece of bread to mask the bitter taste or mix a few drops with her milk and let them fall from her finger tip on to his tongue. Her mother always kept strips of cottonwood bark in the house in case any of the children suffered a fever. Why hadn't she brought any with her? She turned the burro south and listened to the child's torn breaths fall in with the mule's steady pace.

## 9

Gulliver senior reined in his horse and the posse drew to a halt round him. They had been in the saddle all day and had nothing to show for it. The men were exhausted and the horses needed water. Desert dust covered their clothes and was in their eyes and mouths. It was close to the end of daylight now and the colours of the land and sky deepened.

'Where d'you think he's gone, boss?'

Gulliver glared at Tucker.

'We'll head back,' Gulliver said. 'Get some chow inside us, catch a few hours sleep and start again in the morning.'

'There's a ridge away to the east we haven't tried,' Tucker suggested.

The men groaned.

'Ain't enough light left,' Gulliver said.

He wheeled his horse round and the others followed.

Usually, as you climbed the slope to the charcoal camp in the evenings you saw rows of campfires and the yellow light of the men's oil lamps. But tonight, the men had carried their lamps to a part of the camp midway between the tents and where they ate. It took Gulliver a few moments to realize that the men were crowded round the company office. The shadowy beehive shapes of the kilns reared over everything and the smell of burnt wood hung in the air.

'What's going on, boss?' Tucker said.

Gulliver ignored him.

The men were sitting facing the office with their lamps on the ground beside them. Some were sprawled, propped up on an elbow chatting to the guys nearest them. The red dots of their cigarettes glowed like fireflies. Some of them had brought their axes over and were using their whetstones just as they did every evening. They looked round to stare as Gulliver's posse rode in.

Gulliver swung himself down off his horse at the edge of the crowd. He was surprised that none of the men moved aside to let him pass. They were not blocking his path exactly, just not moving to let him through. He strode round the edge of the crowd with Tucker trailing behind. It was then Gulliver realized the foreman Bill Wheeling was on the office porch, standing in front of the door with his .45 in his hand. Gulliver climbed over the men nearest the building.

'What's going on?'

'Boss, the guys have got it into their heads that you stole the payroll,' Wheeling said.

'What?'

Tucker laughed. One of the men stood up. A Mexican.

'Boss?'

Gulliver glowered at him.

'Who are you?'

'Pablo Caborca, boss. You hired me the day the camp opened.'

'Did I?'

Was this Mexican cutter some kind of leader? Had he

87

got them all to do this? Gulliver looked into the faces of the other men. Some of them looked away to avoid his stare.

'What's this about?' Gulliver sneered.

'The guys don't think Lucas took the payroll.'

Caborca was speaking loudly so the others could hear. Tucker's hand was resting on the handle of his Colt.

'That so?' Gulliver feigned surprise.

'None of us would have,' Caborca explained. 'That money belongs to all of us. We got families.'

In the dusk, Caborca's lantern lit his anxious face. Lamps amidst the crowd lit other faces watching him, the ends of cigarettes brightened and faded. Gulliver could see shapes of the men in the shadows, the outline of their hats, their square shoulders. Murmured conversations rose and fell. He could feel them waiting for him to speak.

'We reckoned,' Caborca went on, 'that the only place in the camp that wasn't searched was the foreman's bunkhouse. We reckoned we ought to search it.'

'I wasn't about to let that happen,' Wheeling said. 'The men ain't allowed in the company office.'

'Shut up,' Gulliver said.

He beckoned Caborca up on to the porch.

'Ever seen the payroll?'

Caborca hesitated.

'No, but I guess it's in one of them canvas bags.'

Gulliver took Caborca's lantern and pushed open the office door. He held the lantern so the light shone into the room, the open safe, the table, chairs, the two untidy bunks against the back wall.

'See one of them canvas bags?'

'No boss.'

Gulliver handed him back the lamp and gestured for

him to take his place in the crowd.

'Listen up,' Gulliver said. The buzz of conversation stilled. 'We got a dead man back here we ain't even buried yet. You all know someone came at him from behind.'

Gulliver caught Caborca's eye.

'You believe me about that don't you or do you want to see where his skull is smashed in?'

No one spoke.

'And we got a missing payroll and we got Lucas Redwood on the run.'

Gulliver paused to give weight to his words.

'We found his wife and kid today out in the desert all alone. Looked like she was running for the border.'

Gulliver waited again.

'Where would you say Lucas is headed?'

The men's conversation rose.

'Back to your tents,' Wheeling called. 'Get them axes sharp for the morning.'

The men ignored him and got to their feet. As convincing as Gulliver had been, the men knew something was wrong. Gulliver called out to Caborca.

'Find another couple of guys and get a grave dug at first light.'

He watched the men head back towards the tents, lanterns bobbing in the darkness and turned to Wheeling.

'Why the hell didn't you let 'em search the office?'

Wheeling looked at Tucker.

'It's the office, boss.'

'Get that cook to fix us something,' Gulliver said to Tucker. Then he turned back to Wheeling.

'I'm having your bunk. You're on the floor tonight.' He chuckled to himself. 'Maybe one of the men would let you share his tent.'

Wheeling flinched.

'Floor's fine boss. I'll fix a bed-roll for you while you get something to eat.'

Gulliver led the way down to the chow tent.


'This is your fault.'

Leonard eyed Gulliver junior.

'Those are the security guys from the rail-head,' Gulliver said. 'Must have followed us.'

'You're the boss's son,' Leonard said. 'Go out there and talk to 'em.'

Curly stared out through the smashed glass.

'Anyone takes a step outside that door, they'll shoot him before they can tell who he is,' Gulliver said. 'You know that.'

The heat of late afternoon filled the wooden building. Even though the men were sheltered from the direct attack of the sun, the hot air sapped their strength. Flies drilled at the upper panes of the window.

'You came straight here knowing there was guys follow-ing you?' Leonard said, unwilling to let it go.

He glared at Gulliver.

'There must be four of 'em at least. Probably more coming.'

'We could use the shaft,' McCall said. 'Hide down there.'

Everyone turned to look at him.

'We got about ten minutes before those fellas are here, I reckon.'

'How far back does it go?' Gulliver said.

McCall shrugged.

'Twenty, twenty five yards under the ridge.'

'Where does it come out?'

'Don't come out nowhere. We just stopped digging when the seam ran out.'

Leonard spat on to the wooden floor.

'It's all caved in,' he said. 'Anyone can see that.'

'No it ain't,' McCall said. 'We just blocked the entrance to stop anyone else mining it. Thought we might come back one day.'

'I ain't about to die in a hole in the ground like some rat,' Leonard said.

'There's a ventilation shaft,' McCall said. 'Comes out by a stand of trees on the ridge. It was the last thing we dug before we decided to quit.'

Lucas was on his feet.

'We got to get that entrance unblocked now.'

'Me and Curly are stayin' here,' Leonard said.

'I ain't,' Curly said. 'Minute we run out of ammo, we're crowbait.'

Lucas and Joe McCall heaved rocks out of the mouth of the shaft. Gulliver unhitched the saddle-bags and Curly led the horses away to the shade of trees yards away from the saloon. Leonard paced up and down in the dust. His face was white and his shirt clung to his back, dark with sweat.

'They're gonna know,' he said. 'They'll know you're in there.'

Lucas shifted enough earth and rock to make an entrance. Joe McCall was first to crawl in.

'What's it like?' Lucas called to him.

Curly came running back.

'They're coming.'

Gulliver dived into the hole after Lucas and hauled the saddle-bags after him. Hoof beats sounded on the ridge on the far side of the saloon.

'I can't,' Leonard said simply. His face was bleached with fear. He looked at Curly helplessly. 'I'll take my chances. I'll be able to hold 'em off till Pa gets here.'

The hoofbeats were louder now.

'Please stay with me,' Leonard said simply.

'We don't know when Pa's gonna come,' Curly said. 'You got the Winchester.'

There were shouts of men up on the ridge. The brothers held each other's eyes for a second then Curly scrambled into the opening of the shaft, Leonard leapt up on to the porch of the saloon.

Dirt rained down as Curly edged along the shaft after the others. Airless and damp, the tunnel was barely high enough for him to crawl. In the darkness, root tendrils whipped his face, stones cut his knees and dirt got in his mouth. Some rodent squealed and scampered past him. When his shoulder knocked against a timber prop, dirt and stones cascaded over him. Sweat ran into his eyes. Eventually his hand touched something. A saddle-bag.

'Leonard?' a voice whispered. It was Gulliver.

'It's Curly. Leonard ain't coming.'

As Curly's eyes adjusted, he could make out a patch of daylight up ahead. Now that he was still, the faint breeze between the ventilation hole and the entrance ran over his face.

'There's a chamber,' Gulliver whispered. 'Can't all fit in it. You and me have got to wait in the shaft.'

Curly turned his face to the breeze.

'How long?'

'Till dark,' Gulliver said. 'Then they reckon we can push up through the ventilation shaft and make a break.'

Curly strained to hear what was going on outside but the deaf earth entombed him. All he could hear was blood pounding in his head. He concentrated on the air crossing his face and stayed alert for the sound of dirt raining from the roof.

They could have been there an hour or half an hour, Curly couldn't tell. The darkness swallowed any sense of time. Only the sound of men breathing reminded him he was not alone. Maybe the riders from the rail-head had gone. Maybe they had looked for them and because they hadn't found them, they'd cleared out.

Then there was a disturbance at the entrance to the shaft. Some animal maybe. Curly tensed. Lying flat, he raised his head to look back to the rag of daylight which hung far back in the darkness.

'Cover us with that Winchester,' Gulliver hissed.

'Leonard's got it.'

There was more scrabbling at the entrance of the shaft. They all heard it. Somewhere up past where Gulliver lay someone whispered. It could have been McCall. Curly couldn't catch the words but he picked up the strain in the voice, the fear. Perhaps Leonard had changed his mind and come after them. There hadn't been any shooting, had there? Maybe he had slipped away from the posse. He strained to see. He willed Leonard to come crawling down the shaft. Maybe he had come to tell them that the men had gone. Why didn't he call out?

More daylight: someone had shifted a boulder. Leonard didn't have to do that. He could have crawled round it like they had. He could have called out. They would have heard him. What was he doing?

The sound of the pistol shot was deadened by the earth walls of the tunnel. Curly couldn't tell where it went. He sank himself into the floor of the shaft and willed the dirt to swallow him. Another shot followed. He felt the bullet pass him and heard it slam into the tunnel wall by his head. And there were voices. One of the men laughed. He could see the silhouettes of a man against the daylight at the end of the tunnel as he fired. Then he rolled aside.

Gulliver hissed to get Curly's attention. He passed something to him. A Colt. Curly took aim at the square of light. The outline of a man's hat filled the square for a second. Curly squeezed the trigger. It gave slightly then stuck hard. Dirt had clogged the chamber. Curly squeezed again. Nothing.

'Darker than the ace of spades up there,' a voice said. 'Can't tell if they're in there or not.'

'I ain't going in to find out,' another voice said. 'Give 'em one more and we'll seal it up.'

The pistol cracked again. Curly felt a hot steel wire run through his thigh and heard the slug thud into the tunnel wall. He grabbed the wound and his lungs bucked as he fought to stop himself crying out. The steel wire had melted in his leg and left barbs embedded in the flesh. His leg, his hands and the earth on which he lay were slippery and wet.

The daylight disappeared. There was muffled banging at the tunnel entrance as someone hammered rocks in place. Curly lay back. The draught which had given him some relief had gone. In its place, the pain in his thigh burned him like a brand.

Gulliver said 'You hit?'

Curly groaned. His head rested on the saddle-bags which held the silver.

# 10

'Who's going first?'

It had been dark for an hour. Through the ventilation hole they could see the starry sky.

'Not me,' Curly said. 'I can't run on this leg.'

'I'll go,' Lucas said.

'I'll be right behind you,' Gulliver said. 'Your gun still work?'

Lucas handed him his Colt.

'Let me carry the silver.'

Lucas held out his hand for the bags.

'Ain't riskin' you taking off on your own,' Gulliver said. Get down there and untie the horses.'

'Ain't heard that brother of yours using that rifle,' McCall said.

'He's smart,' Curly said. 'He'll be hiding out on the ridge somewhere. He'll start shooting as soon as you make a break for it.'

Lucas pushed up through the ventilation hole. Dirt showered over his face.

'Get down to the railway line and head south,' Curly said. 'Next town is Pinyonville. That's where Pa will be with the money.'

'That's a day's ride,' Gulliver snapped. 'He was supposed to meet me here.'

'You were supposed to come alone.'

Lucas tore away the sides of the narrow shaft and heaved himself out on to the ridge. Cold night air bathed his face and tasted sweet in his mouth. He kept low expecting someone to be covering him with a Colt. But there was no one. Below him, outside the saloon, the guards from the rail-head were sitting round a fire. On the porch lay the body of a man with a Winchester beside him. Away to the left, under the trees, their horses were still tethered.

Lucas inched forward on his belly and lay still every few yards. He could hear the crackle and spit of the fire and the murmured conversation of the men. Gulliver was tight behind him, gasping for breath with the effort of dragging the heavy bags.

Lucas let himself down amongst the horses by a branch of one of the cottonwoods and unhitched the reins. As the animals shifted, he could see the backs of the men round the fire. None of them turned.

Gulliver and Joe McCall peered over the lip of the ridge. Sensing the men above them, the horses stamped and pulled. The voices of the men were suddenly louder. Someone called out.

'We got to break for it now,' Gulliver hissed.

Hearing Gulliver scramble down the side of the ridge, holding the saddle-bags, Lucas swung himself up into the saddle. His axe was still secured with leather laces. There was shouting from the direction of the saloon, the sound of running. A pistol shot cracked in the night air, then another. When Lucas glanced back, one of the men was taking aim at him, supporting his pistol with two hands. Lucas urged his horse forward. Gulliver shouted something. Joe McCall was still on the ridge, maybe Curly was with him, Lucas couldn't tell. Another shot sang through the night, then another. He spurred his horse on. He had to get out of range.

The desert floor jumped like a drumskin under the horse's hoofs. The animal's mane whipped Lucas's face and the night air stung his eyes. The horse powered past contorted shadows, misshapen boulders, over a mile of iron dirt and stony ground. Moonlight caught the spines on the beaver tail and silhouetted the sharp bladed yucca trees. Lucas rode to where darkness promised to hide him.

Eventually, he slowed his horse and wheeled to let the others catch up. There was no one behind him. He strained to hear the sound of hoof beats but there was silence. He peered into the darkness but saw only the star paved sky and the silver land. A coyote howled somewhere far away.

What had happened to them? Gulliver had been right behind him on the ridge. The rail-head guards must have them pinned down. Lucas hesitated. Go on or go back? He could ride on to Pinyonville then the border. No one would catch him now. Maria and the child would already be at Angel Pass. They were safe, no one knew who they were. All three of them could cross together just like they planned and be safe in Maria's village in two days.

Empty handed. Lucas would be taking nothing for Maria and nothing for the child. The people of the village were already hungry: Maria, Lucas and the child would just be three more mouths to feed. And the guy with the money wouldn't wait in Pinyonville forever. Lucas had to find him. Together they would go back for the silver and make the exchange. He would take his share, pay off Joe McCall and after that he would head for the border.

*

'Can't take neither of you after what happened yesterday.'

At first light, Gulliver senior sat at the foremen's table with Tucker and Wheeling.

'Needs two of you here. Just keep the men working, it'll keep their minds off this Lucas fella.'

As light rose in the sky, the three men finished their breakfast and pushed their plates away across the table. The cutters shivered in the queue for food.

'I'll ride into Ponderosa and get the sheriff to gather up a posse. I like to deal with things myself but this time I reckon it's best to hand it on to him.'

'You gonna tell the men before you leave?'

'About the Chinese cutters?'

Gulliver drew a stogie out of his waistcoat pocket. He bit off the end and spat it on to the ground.

'If I tell 'em now they won't want to work today.'

Gulliver lit the cigar.

'We find Lucas, we find the payroll. I'll pay the men and tell 'em there ain't no more work for 'em at the same time. If they're holding their pay they won't argue. They don't have to know about the Chinese workers taking over.'

The smoke from the stogie made Gulliver cough.

'What about if there's trouble?' Wheeling kept his voice low. 'Like yesterday.'

The cook started serving the men's food. The line moved quickly and the morning air smelled of beans and pork fat.

'What are you worried about?' Gulliver said.

His eyes hardened.

'The Mexican,' Wheeling said. 'Caborca. He's a troublemaker.'

'We can take care of him,' Tucker said. He kicked Wheeling under the table.

'He's a talker,' Wheeling insisted. 'Gets the others riled up. If he was on his own we could take care of him.'

'He the one reckoned I stole my own payroll?' Gulliver said.

Wheeling nodded.

'If you'd let him into the office, there wouldn't have been no trouble,' Gulliver said. 'It wasn't him caused that trouble, it was you.'

'We got to get the teams moving,' Tucker said. 'We don't want no late start.'

He looked at Gulliver to see his reaction. Gulliver was watching the men. They were already getting to their feet. Tucker stood up and cupped his hands round his mouth.

'Same teams as yesterday,' he called. 'Same teams as yesterday. Start where you finished last night.'

The men looked away from him and made their way back to their tents.

'They knew that,' Wheeling said.

Tucker glared at him.

'Tell you what I'll do,' Gulliver said. 'I'll take Caborca with me.'

Tucker and Wheeling stared at him.

'Can't cause trouble if he's riding with the sheriff's posse. Besides, he might know where Lucas is.'

Gulliver drew on his stogie and smiled.

'That solve your problem, boys?'


Inside an hour, Gulliver and Caborca stood in the sheriff's office in Ponderosa. Hans Birkmeir was sheriff and town blacksmith. The office was next door to the forge and he walked over with blackened hands still wearing his apron when he saw Gulliver and Caborca arrive. In the five years Birkmeir had been sheriff, he had never once had cause to raise a posse.

'Who am I gonna call on?' Birkmeir said. 'Men round here got work to do. They don't want to go chasing round after outlaws. Anyhow, most of 'em are working up at your charcoal camp.'

'There must be someone,' Gulliver said.

'There's only Charlie from the saloon or old Buck from the livery stable. Why didn't you use your men from the charcoal camp?'

'Can't spare no one,' Gulliver said. 'Production's falling behind.'

'Can't the two of you go after him?' Birkmeir said. 'It's only one man and I just got the forge fired up. Who are you after anyway?'

Gulliver told him.

'Lucas?' Birkmeir said.

'Where do you think he might have went?' Gulliver said.

'You're telling me Lucas done this?'

Amazement echoed in the sheriff's voice.

'Reckon he's hiding out round here somewhere,' Gulliver said. 'Most likely headed for the border in a couple of days,'

'Killed Gus Hobbs and ran off with the payroll?' Birkmeir said, shaking his head. 'You got proof?'

'The men don't believe he done it,' Caborca said.

He had been quiet up until then. Birkmeir eyed him sharply.

'Hobbs is dead with his skull split open,' Gulliver snapped. 'Money's gone and this man's run off. What more proof do you need?'

Birkmeir considered.

'Anyhow, he'll have the payroll with him,' Gulliver added. 'Or he'll have hidden it.'

'Guess it wouldn't do no harm to bring him in,' Birkmeir said. 'Could try Red Tail.'

'The old mine workings?' Gulliver said. 'Does anyone go up there now?'

'Saloon's still got a roof on it,' Birkmeir said. 'Usually some low life hiding out from what I heard.'

'He's a strong guy, this fella we're after,' Gulliver said. 'It'll take three of us.'

'Fill your canteens,' Birkmeir said.

With the sun climbing the sky, the three men rode out of town. Up ahead a hawk wheeled and circled and the morning air smelled of heat.

'I dug that shaft at Red Tail when I was a young man,' Gulliver said. 'Me and a fella called Joe McCall.'

'Nothing left up there now,' Birkmeir said.

'Thought we was gonna build a town up there then the seam ran out. Moved on and tried somewhere else. Got lucky eventually.'

'McCall your partner?' Birkmeir said.

'Joe ain't the ambitious sort,' Gulliver said. 'Never took a risk in his life. Just does what he's told, day in day out. Some fellas are like that.'

Maria shredded the soft inner flesh of a piece of cotton wood bark into a pan where water boiled over a fire. The child lay in the basket in the shade of the tree under the lightest piece of cloth. Each breath racked him. The air rattled in his throat and sucked at his lungs under his ribs. He stared up at the moving leaves too exhausted to cry out. His face was damp and colourless around the mouth.

Sitting on the ground beside the child, Maria watched him as she worked. She brought each shred of bark to her lips to taste and threw aside any that contained any hint of the bitter outer bark. Beside her were a pile of the youngest leaves she could find on the cotton wood tree, pale, almost transparent. After she had made the tincture she would boil them too and when the water had cooled, bathe the child.

The sun was high and molten air surrounded her. A few hours ago Maria worried about the riders catching up with them again, but now she thought only of the child. The world had distilled to this circle of shade under the cotton wood tree. Everything important was here, her love for their child, the potential for life, the closeness of death. Let the riders come.

Somewhere up ahead, where the midday heat bent the air, was Pinyonville. Lucas rode slowly, his hat pulled down low. The sun scourged his shoulders through his thin shirt and as he had emptied his canteen hours before, he tasted desert sand in his mouth. Dazed by the ferocious heat, Lucas let his horse walk slowly on beside the steel rails which aimed straight at the horizon.

As the shapes of wooden buildings appeared in the twisting air, Lucas noticed something else. A rider was approaching and the sunlight flashed off something in his hand. The man was covering him with a .45.

'Come far, fella?'

The rider's eyes were shaded by the brim of his hat and his heavy moustache covered his mouth. A steel watch chain looped between the pockets of his waistcoat and his gun-belt supported twin Peacemakers. He held the reins of his horse in thin fingered hands.

'Ridin' since before sun-up,' Lucas said.

The man watched him.

'Looking out for someone that should be coming from the same direction,' he said.

'Gotta get in the shade,' Lucas said. 'Fill my canteen.'

'Saloon's less than a mile. I'll ride with you.'

Inside the Pinyonville saloon, Lucas took a seat in the shadows away from the door but even here there was no relief from the afternoon heat. A group of men concentrated on a euchre game at another table and the rider fetched a pitcher of water.

'Emmet Jackson,' the man held out his hand to Lucas.

Lucas gulped the water too hard and caught his breath.

'You heard of me?' Jackson watched him.

'Come from Red Tail to look for you,' Lucas said. 'You expecting Gulliver junior?'

'Why should I be?' Jackson said.

'Working for him,' Lucas said.

Lucas told Jackson what had happened.

'My boys?'

'Curly took a bullet in the leg.'

Jackson's face froze.

'Leonard?'

'We should get back out there,' Lucas said. 'Those railroad guys got them out gunned.'

'Leonard's a good shot with a rifle,' Jackson said. 'Just give him a clear line of sight.'

'I left hours ago,' Lucas said. 'Can't say what we'll find.'

'You sure Gulliver's got the silver? I ain't getting into no gunfight if there ain't nothing to fight for.'

Lucas got to his feet. He thought of Joe McCall. The last sight he had had of him was his worried face peering over the ridge in the moonlight.

'You got the money?'

Jackson glared at him.

'I need to get paid,' Lucas insisted.

'Wouldn't be much point in me being here without it.'

'Get me something to eat,' Lucas stretched his legs out on a chair. 'Get the canteens filled and we'll start out right away. And there's one more thing.'

'What?'

'I'm going to need one of your Colts.'

# 11

The colours of the day had deepened by the time Lucas and Emmet Jackson reached Red Tail. The desert slipped from ochre to rust and the sky from violet to indigo. Ahead of them, starlight glittered on a vein of quartz crystals in the ridge behind the old saloon and a night breeze disturbed the leaves of the cottonwoods.

'Reckon one of us should circle round?' Jackson said.

'Horses are gone,' Lucas said. 'Maybe they lit out.'

The men watched for a movement in the saloon doorway or under the trees but there was none.

'Give me one of your Colts,' Lucas said. 'I'll get up on to the ridge.'

He galloped off to where the land sloped down to the plain.

Jackson walked his horse forward a few yards and kept his eyes on the saloon door. A shadow moved on the porch. Jackson reined in and stood still. A piece of darkness shifted just beneath the window, only a slight movement but Jackson was sure he had seen something. Then he realized what it was and his belly turned to water. He had to get up close and see. It couldn't be one of the boys, they could look after themselves. Leonard was a good shot, just give him a clear line of sight and Curly would do whatever his brother told him. He urged his horse forward and at the sound of the hoof beats, a turkey vulture lumbered off the porch and hopped away a few yards. Jackson leapt down off his horse and ran towards what he now saw was a body on the saloon porch. There was a Winchester lying beside it. The vulture adjusted its wings and settled to watch him.

'Anybody there?' Jackson called.

His Colt was in his hand now. No answer. No movement from inside the saloon. There must be someone here. Thoughts skittled into each other inside his head. He knew who the body was. He didn't look at it. He couldn't. The gun shook in his hand. He turned and fired at the bird. Then he fired again. The vulture skipped aside, stretched its wings and levered itself gracelessly into the air. Then he heard a horse above him on the ridge and Lucas call out.

Jackson climbed up on the porch keeping his eyes off the body and stepped into the saloon. For a second the darkness blinded him.

'Anyone here?'

Then shadows emerged from the darkness, chairs, tables the oak bar covered with dust. Jackson's boot heels echoed against the floorboards.

'Anyone here?'

He stepped outside into the silver light again and kept his gaze away from the body.

'Lucas?'

Lucas appeared on the ridge above him.

'They're all dead.'

'All of 'em?' Jackson's voice caught in his throat. 'What about Curly?'

106

'You better get up here.'

Jackson heaved himself on to the ridge by way of the branches of the cottonwood. The vulture squatted a little distance away from the saloon and waited for him to leave.

The ridge was a battlefield. Bodies were strewn in the dust. Gulliver still had a Colt in his hand, his shirt front was dark with blood and vultures had pecked out his eyes. Jackson saw Curly's body staring blindly at him and looked away. Lucas knelt beside Joe McCall. He spoke to him softly, straightened his arms and legs which had twisted as he fell and adjusted his shirt so the line of buttons ran straight. There were bodies of other men who Lucas didn't recognize, the railroad guards from Plataville. They lay where the crossfire had caught them, wrenched their bodies and splayed their limbs. Jackson stared out across the plain and refused to look at any of it. His movements were stiff and his face was grave.

'Who's that?'

'Joe McCall. I was gonna give him half my share.'

'You and him were partners?'

'Kinda. He drove a wagon up at the smelting works. Been around silver mines a long time.'

'I started out as a working man,' Jackson reflected. 'Picking bauxite off the desert floor in the heat of the day. Even dug holes in the ground for John Gulliver for a while.'

Jackson kicked a stone off the edge of the ridge and listen to it rattle down the roof of the saloon.

'Learned one thing,' Jackson continued. 'Never trust no one with more money than you. They either took it off you or took it before you got there.'

'All Joe wanted was a place of his own so he could sit out in the air with a fishing pole,' Lucas said.

'Where's the silver?' Jackson said. 'That's what we come for.'

In the west, the sun was dipping towards the horizon and away to the east the cobalt sky darkened into night. Lucas lay face down on the ground and reached into the ventilation shaft. He hauled up one set of saddle-bags and then the other. Jackson unlaced the flaps and peered inside. He lifted out a silver bar and held it up in the dying light. The letters JG were stamped in the corner.

'We gonna bury 'em?' Lucas looked around.

'Ground's too hard for grave diggin',' Jackson said.

'They're your boys.'

'They were men,' Jackson said quietly. 'They made their choice just like me. You either spend your life working for Gulliver like your friend Joe McCall or you find another way. That's what I taught 'em.'

Jackson glanced over to where the bodies lay and sighed wearily.

'Came out the same in the end.'

'We can't leave 'em for the vultures,' Lucas said.

Jackson appeared not to hear him. Stone faced and silent, he stared out across the empty desert. Grief pulled him into himself and he was indifferent to anything that happened around him. Eventually, when he did speak, his voice caught in his throat.

'You got a kid?' he said.

'A boy.' Lucas smiled. 'Still a baby.'

'What will you want him to do? Work for someone like Gulliver or take his chances?'

'We should bury 'em,' Lucas said.

'We'll put 'em in the shaft and seal it up.'

It took Lucas and Jackson an hour to lower the bodies through the ventilation shaft and find enough rocks to make a strong seal. Jackson moved as if his joints were stiff like an old man's and the effort was too much for him. Silver moonlight cast long shadows from the roof of the saloon and the branches of the cottonwoods.

'You want to say a few words?' Lucas said.

'Talked to my boys every day of their lives,' Jackson said. 'Ain't got nothin' new to tell 'em right now.' His voice was hoarse and he was stooped as if he carried a corn sack across his shoulders. His steps faltered and he looked as if he might fall.

Jackson threw down the saddle-bags and the two men scrambled down off the ridge, supporting themselves on the branches of the cottonwoods. It was too late to ride on. Lucas lifted the saddle off his horse and spread out his bed-roll. Jackson started to gather kindling for a fire but after a few moments, Lucas noticed him staring out into the darkness with sticks in his hand as if he had forgotten what he was doing. Lucas made a fire and stood a coffee pot next to the flames.

'Guess we better do the exchange now.'

Jackson opened his own saddle-bag and held out two canvass bags with the name of the bank stencilled on them.

'I'll take one,' Lucas said. 'Half share was the deal I made.'

Jackson stared at him.

'I'm takin' all the silver.'

Lucas stuffed the bank-bag under his saddle.

'My son might ask me one day. What would I tell him?'

'Tell him you took it from a man who had too much,' Jackson said. 'Tell him you took it from a man you worked for who owed you more than he paid.'

'Have to tell him I took it,' Lucas said, 'not earned it.'

Jackson stared into the fire and sipped his coffee.

Lucas climbed into his bed-roll and fell asleep while he was trying to work out how far he was from the border.

At first light, Jackson shook Lucas awake. The eastern sky was the colour of water in which someone had rinsed blood off his hands.

'Riders coming.'

Hoofbeats sounded from the direction of Pinyonville. Lucas gathered up his bed-roll.

'Help me hide the silver,' Jackson said. 'They catch us with that, we're dead men.'

Lucas levered a rock out from the mouth of the ventilation shaft while Jackson dropped the bags inside. Lucas rammed the rock back in place and they both kicked dust over it. Someone might think it had been sealed for a while. They could see the riders now: three horses, their heads down low coming at a hard gallop. A red dust cloud glittered behind them.

'You told anyone you were coming here?' Jackson said.

Lucas shook his head.

'If we start now, we've got half an hour on them,' Jackson said. 'Best split up.'

'I'll head south,' Lucas said.

'Just make sure you don't double back and try to dig up that silver.'

'The men heaved their saddles up on to the horses.

'What about you?' Lucas said.

Jackson shrugged.

'North I guess.'

Lucas mounted up and rode out across the desert with the sun on his left hand. The further away from Red Tail he rode, the lighter his heart became. The border was only

110

a day away, a day and a half at most. Maria would already be there. He reached round and ran his hand over the saddle-bags. He had the money. He even had Jackson's pistol stuffed in his belt. What could go wrong? He just had to keep ahead of the men and make sure he didn't overtire his horse. When he looked back, Emmet Jackson hadn't moved. He was sitting astride his mount up on the Red Tail ridge staring after him.

Lucas realized he should be making plans. What if it was Gulliver with some kind of posse who was following? What if he did catch up with him? He'd tell him the truth. What else could he do? It had been an accident. Pablo Caborca would back him up. Maybe someone else at the camp saw what happened too.

As sunlight spread across the sky, a lone hawk circled. The flat, stony ground spread in front of him and as he rode the tide of his thoughts changed. What good would telling the truth do? If Pablo was going to stand up for him, he would have done it by now. No one else had seen what had happened. By running away, he had handed them proof of his guilt. Gulliver would fire Caborca and believe what he wanted to believe.

Lucas looked back again. The riders had reached Red Tail and were grouped outside the saloon looking up at the ridge. Jackson was still astride his horse. His arm was outstretched, pointing in Lucas's direction.

Tucker and Wheeling were at their usual table outside the chow tent. They mopped their breakfast plates with hunks of bread as the queue of cutters filed past them. The burners had just unsealed a kiln and the smell of charcoal hung in the air like dirt. The mountain slope shielded the camp from the warmth of the morning sun and mist clung to the pines.

'Hey Tucker, any news?'

Three men stood in front of Wheeling and Tucker. The foremen looked up, surprised because the men rarely approached them. Wheeling recognized them as the ones who wouldn't let him sit with them two nights ago.

'Any news about Lucas?'

'They'll catch him,' Tucker said. 'Mr Gulliver don't give up on nothing.'

He expected the group of men to walk away then. He had given them an answer.

'You reckon Lucas done it?' the man persisted.

Wheeling seemed to see him properly then. It was the one who had suggested Gulliver had stolen his own money. He was short with a compact, muscular frame like a boxer. Wheeling still couldn't remember his name so he let Tucker do the talking.

'Run off didn't he?' Tucker said.

'Could have got scared because he thought someone might pin something on him.'

'Don't look like it to me,' Tucker said.

The man turned to Wheeling.

'What about you, boss?' he said. 'You heard anything?'

'No,' Wheeling said.

'You reckon he done it too?'

'I guess.'

Wheeling looked away from the man. The embarrassment of two nights ago came back to him. Why had the man called him boss? No one called him that.

'The guys still don't reckon he done it,' the man said. 'They reckon Gulliver's got it wrong. The men know Lucas wouldn't do nothing like that.'

'Listen Henry,' Tucker said. 'There's a killing and a

robbery and one guy out of the whole camp runs off. You're telling me he didn't do it?'

'That's right,' the man said. 'Lucas just ain't like that.'

The man turned to Wheeling.

'Hear that? Hear what he called me?'

Wheeling nodded.

'You ain't lookin' at me,' the man said. 'What's my second name?'

The men all stared at him. Tucker started to say something.

'Wait,' the man said. 'Let him answer.'

Wheeling hesitated.

'Meadows.' The man leaned over the table towards Wheeling. 'Henry Meadows.'

Wheeling clambered awkwardly back over the bench and stood up purple-faced.

'Been working here ten months,' Meadows said. 'I told you the other night.'

'Bet he can't even remember his own name,' someone said.

Everyone laughed. Even Tucker.

'You ain't going to be working here much longer,' Wheeling burst out. 'Mr Gulliver is gonna can the whole lot of you.'

The whole camp seemed to go quiet. The men in the chow line and everyone at the tables turned towards him.

'He don't mean that,' Tucker said quietly.

'Don't he?' Meadows said.

He turned to Wheeling.

'What d'you mean, boss?'

'Mr Gulliver is gonna get Chinese cutters from San Francisco, that's what,' Wheeling yelled. 'Gonna pay 'em half what he pays you.'

113

Wheeling's words fell like an axe. He looked into the faces of the men.

'He says he ain't making no profits because the payroll costs too much.'

There was a moment while the men took in what they had heard. Wheeling couldn't stop. He couldn't tell if he had said too much or not enough but he had to finish.

'He came up to tell you,' he crowed. 'Then Lucas stole the payroll. He didn't get the chance.'

Meadows turned to Tucker.

'This true?'

'I don't know. . . .' Tucker stumbled over his words.

'These Chinese fellas, they bringin' their own foremen with 'em?' Meadows said.

'You think Mr Gulliver would trust a Chinese foreman?' Wheeling yelled.

Tucker grabbed Wheeling's arm to shut him up but it was too late.

'He's giving us the can and he's keeping you on?' Meadows said. His voice fell away in disbelief.

Wheeling laughed.

Meadows and the others stared at Wheeling for a moment and saw what he said was most likely true. There was no point in arguing. They turned their backs on the foremen and made their way up the hill towards where the tents were pitched.

'Production's falling, what do you expect?' Wheeling yelled after them.

The other men filed past as if they hadn't heard and chatted to each other just as they did on their way to work every morning. Except that today they took care to look away from the two foremen and step round their table as if the air was contaminated.

As the cutters passed the office, someone punched the wooden wall. Someone else joined in with a kick. Then the door was pushed open and someone threw a stone through the window. Then one of the big guys who worked the two handed saws came along and shouldered the hut so that it rocked on its frail foundations. Others joined in. Then with the sound of splitting timber, the hut was on its side.

Someone shouted something about foremen having to sleep in tents like the Chinese cutters now. There were gales of laughter from the crowd. Men ran back from the rows of tents to join in. Men kicked the cottonwood planks until they splintered, the door was thrown aside. A couple of guys heaved the open safe across the ground. Papers, ledgers, bed-rolls and clothes were thrown up into the air. Then there was a shout which cut through the noise and laughter. It was Henry Meadows's voice.

'Look at this, fellas. I found something.'

He turned to the crowd of men like a fair-ground prize-winner, a mile-wide grin slapped across his face. Held high above his head was the bulging canvas bank-bag which everyone recognized as the payroll.

# 12

The riders who followed Lucas were in no hurry. Heading south, they guessed he would take the short cut off the playa and they knew he would have to rest his horse when the heat of the day came. They were easy on their own horses, conserving their strength for when Lucas slowed.

Here, the fault line which bordered the playa had thrown up a long rise of peaks which rose abruptly from the desert floor. At the lower edges, apart from ragged patches of creosote bush, clumps of barrel cacti and the occasional wind blown yucca which had managed to take root, the ground was loose stones or bare rock. Above the bajadas, bitter bush, elderberry and mahonia clung to the mountain side. Deer tracks wound between the boulders.

Freshwater Canyon was the short cut. The other way off the playa was to circle the peaks which meant an extra day's ride. Freshwater was a mile long, zigzag fissure in the rock, ten yards wide at the entrance which narrowed to allowing only a single horse to pass at its mid point where a spring broke through. Water bubbled into a pool but as soon as it flowed out of the shadows, it dried up on the baked earth. In the rock wall opposite the spring, a swathe of pale crystals was worn smooth through use as a deer

116

lick. The border was half a day's ride the other side.

Lucas slipped out of his saddle at the canyon entrance. He grabbed the reins of his horse and led it up a sandy track away from the opening. The prints of mule deer and black tails which had come down to drink, carpeted the path together with the prints of the coyotes and bobcats which had followed them. He climbed until a ledge gave him a view of the playa and the mouth of the pass and there was a yucca to provide shade for his horse. He kept his eyes on the dust cloud kicked up by the riders, pulled the Colt out of his belt and settled down to wait.

Two of them. Back at Red Tail there had been three. Lucas shaded his eyes, scanned the plain and peered along the edge of the ridge. Was there some other pass or some track over the mountains the third rider had taken to cut him off? The sun was high now and the heat of the day bounced off the desert floor and the walls of rock. Lucas spun the chamber of the Colt. He had never shot a man. The dust cloud was getting closer. He lay down behind a gap between two rocks and concentrated on the clear view of the entrance to the pass.

Lucas couldn't recognize either of the riders at this distance. Which one should he shoot first? Lucas felt a line of sweat prick his forehead. Another few yards and they would be within range. If they entered the pass, they would wait for him where the walls of rock narrowed and shoot him as he rode in. His heart crashed in his chest but his hand was steady. He pulled back the hammer of the Colt, squinted along the sight and covered the canyon entrance. He would shoot the first one to approach. His finger tightened on the trigger.

After a minute, Lucas looked back. The riders had reined in their horses, sat beside each other and stared into the entrance to the canyon. They were arguing, probably about who should go first. Lucas could see who they were now. Gulliver and Pablo Coborca. Why had Caborca come after him? Had he told them what had happened and come to persuade Lucas to give himself up? Had he told them Lucas would be heading for the border, that Maria would be waiting? Gulliver would never have brought him along unless he had a good reason. From here he could see Caborca was unarmed.

Gulliver drew his pistol. He waved it towards the pass. He was shouting now. Lucas could hear his voice but not what he said. Caborca stared straight ahead. Gulliver leaned across and slapped Caborca's horse behind the saddle, but Caborca held the reins firm and the horse stayed still. Caborca turned to Gulliver. Maybe he said something, Lucas couldn't tell. Gulliver raised his gun then and the shot echoed in the mouth of the pass.

It took Lucas a second to realize. Caborca doubled over in the saddle. Lucas fired then and saw his bullet kick up a pinch of dirt. Gulliver looked up, wildly searching the cliff to see where the shots were coming from. Lucas fired again. Gulliver fired back without aiming and his shot ricocheted off a rock away to the left. After Lucas's third shot, Gulliver wheeled his horse, fired wildly over his shoulder and thundered back the way he had come.

Lucas scrambled down the rocky path and ran to where Caborca lay in the dirt. His thin shirt was soaked in blood. Lucas knelt over him.

'Lucas?' Caborca said.

Lucas tore away the sleeve of his shirt and twisted it tight to make a tourniquet. Gulliver's bullet had smashed a bone in the upper arm. Caborca flinched as his body absorbed the pain. His eyes closed. Maybe he had passed

118

out. Lucas tore branches off a creosote bush to make splints. The dust cloud which followed Gulliver's horse was half a mile north now.

As he released the tourniquet, Caborca flinched again and his eyelids flickered. But there was less bleeding. Lucas bound the sticks to Caborca's arm and looped a sling round his neck with strips of his own shirt.

'Can you ride?' Lucas said.

Caborca groaned. Lucas hauled him to his feet and lifted him into the saddle. He was clearly going to fall. Lucas grabbed the reins of his own horse in one hand, climbed up behind Caborca and held him. He urged the horse towards the mouth of the pass.

As Lucas glanced back, he saw that Gulliver's dust cloud had disappeared. He couldn't have gone beyond the horizon already. He must have stopped. Why had he ridden away so fast? He need only have circled round and stayed out of range. Had he met up with someone? Was there a posse following? Caborca slumped forward unconscious.

The walls of rock towered above them as they entered the pass. Lucas's eyes adjusted to the shadows. Etched into the rock were drawings of men running with spears and men on horseback chasing buffalo watched over by the staring faces of imaginary creatures. Lucas recognized the scenes of hunting, the fluid drawings of men in pursuit of animals to provide for the tribe. But these other faces with their cavernous eyes and bird beaks or wolf snouts were incomprehensible to him.

In the grey light toward the midpoint of the canyon, the horses' hoof fall echoed over the gurgle of running water. The men came to where a spring framed by bright lichen broke through a crack in the rock face and fell into a pool.

119

Lucas dismounted and lifted Pablo Caborca down. The horses bowed their heads to drink. Lucas sat Caborca against the rock wall and offered him water from his cupped hands. As Caborca drank, his eyes opened.

The pass was so narrow here that only a line of sky showed overhead and the shadows turned the place from midday to dusk. High up in the rock face above the spring there was the drawing of an eagle in flight, its wings out-stretched, heading south.

'Leave me here,' Caborca said.

He looked up at Lucas. His eyes were bright with pain and his voice scratched in his throat.

'Gulliver reckons you killed that guy and took the payroll. He just wants to kill you now. You got to leave me, you got to ride fast.'

Half a day's ride to Angel Pass, Lucas thought. Caborca was right; at this pace he was sure to be caught.

Astride his horse, Jackson watched Lucas gallop away to the south and the group of riders close in from the west. Grief for his boys weighed on him like a lead coat, making a run for it was out of the question. Let the riders come. Nothing mattered now. He saw Lucas stop and turn to look back. He could have taken all the money, Jackson thought. What kind of man refuses that?

Early day sunlight pulled colours into the plain. Miles of flat dirt stretched in front of him strewn with cacti and scrub grass. Jackson remembered the first mule train he had followed out to the centre of the desert years before. It had been a morning like this, the thin light, the cool hour before heat made the air sing. The mules halted by a mountain of sacks filled with hard white bauxite and the driver and a boy began to load the animals. The foreman handed each man thirty hessian sacks and a bottle of water sealed with a plug of paper and pointed them in the direction of the bauxite deposits, pale shadows on the distant desert floor. Full sacks to be brought back here by sunset. One of the labourers died of heatstroke on the first day.

Jackson had come out west as a young man and that was what he had come to. Right then he vowed that no son of his was ever going to break his back in the desert for a dollar a day. After a few months, when he asked for a raise and explained that ten cents a sack didn't give him enough money to keep his wife and two young sons, the foreman gave his job to another man. Since that time, apart from a spell working in the silver mines, he had made his own way.

When his thoughts turned to Leonard and Curly, Jackson felt dazed. Right from when they were young, Curly had followed where Leonard led. Leonard always made out he was fearless while Curly never pretended. They were who they were. At the back of his mind, Jackson always feared that things would turn out bad in the end. Could it have been different? They had grown up with him ducking out of sight of the sheriff, holing up in the backrooms of bars, making them keep their counsel about what they had seen. He used to pride himself that he had brought up his boys to keep one step ahead. If they had done time dragging sacks of white crystal across the desert floor under the burning sun would it have given Leonard a sense of caution, would it have made Curly more determined? Would they be alive now?

Jackson poured oily coffee into a tin cup.

Lucas was miles away now. The puff of dust which followed his horse was barely visible as the air moved in the gathering heat. But the other riders were close, their hoof beats drummed steady and relentless and Jackson knew their eyes were fixed on him. He swigged his coffee and waited.

When riders reined in their horses in front of the saloon, Jackson recognized Gulliver and the sheriff of Ponderosa immediately. They had a Mexican with them who he didn't know.

'Lookin' for a fella named Lucas Redwood,' Gulliver called up to him. 'Big, strong guy. Can't mistake him.'

It was obvious that Gulliver didn't know who Jackson was.

'John Gulliver, ain't it?' Jackson said.

'Looking for a fella named Lucas Redwood,' Gulliver repeated, irritation in his voice.

'Do you know me?' Jackson said.

'Why?' Gulliver said. 'Did you work for me?'

'You remember my name?'

'I can't remember the name of everyone who works for me,' Gulliver snapped. 'Seen this fella or ain't you?'

'I know you,' the sheriff said. He slid his .45 out of its holster. 'Emmet Jackson. You're a wanted man in San Francisco, you and your two hoodlum boys. There's a reward out for you.'

'Just run into the guy you're after,' Jackson said quickly.

He raised his arm and pointed into the far distance at the dust kicked up by Lucas's horse. Gulliver and the Mexican turned to look.

'Toss your gun down,' Sheriff Birkmeir snapped.

He pulled back the hammer on his Colt.

Jackson threw his gun into the sand as if he didn't care one way or the other.

'Climb down on the roof of the saloon and let yourself down easy.'

122

When Jackson was on the ground, the sheriff dismounted. His gun was leveled at Jackson's chest.

'I ain't got time for this,' Gulliver snapped.

Jackson turned to Gulliver.

'My name is Emmet Jackson. I worked beside you for ten months down the shaft at the Fire Creek mine. Couldn't keep my family on the wages you paid.'

Gulliver stared at him, nonplussed.

'Fire Creek was years ago. A lot of men worked for me since then.'

'You and Caborca go on ahead,' the sheriff said.

He swung his Colt and caught Jackson on the jaw. Jackson's legs crumpled under him.

'Ain't letting this one get away.'

Gulliver nodded to Caborca and wheeled his horse around.

'Bound to be headed for the shortcut through Freshwater,' Gulliver said. 'That takes him direct to the border. Ain't no hurry now. He'll have to rest his horse. You'll have time to catch up with me.'

Gulliver spurred his horse and waved Caborca to follow.

'He'll wait for you in the canyon,' the sheriff called after him. 'Take a good look before you ride in there.'

Jackson groaned and blood welled from the corner of his mouth. Birkmeir reached into his saddle-bag and produced a pair of handcuffs. He rolled Jackson over, locked his hands behind his back and dragged him up against one of the posts which supported the saloon porch.

The glassy air closed round Gulliver and Caborca. Beyond them, Lucas's dust cloud headed straight for Freshwater. No hurry, the sheriff thought. He turned to Jackson. His eyes were open and dirt clung to the blood round his mouth.

'You gonna tell me what you're doing out here,' the sheriff said. 'Or am I gonna have to beat it out of you?'

# 13

Angel Pass was high above the tree line where the ground levelled and humidity deepened the scent of the ever-greens. Two wing-shaped slabs of stone at least a hundred feet high towered over the pines. They were lustrous blue black in the shade but as the sun moved, rock crystals bedded in the surface of the slabs glittered like fire. A tongue of flame appeared to curl across each of the stones from sun rise to sun set. The track which climbed up from the playa floor crossed the plateau and led between the stones. Beside them, a clearing had been made and a cantina was built there.

Patches of mud plaster had fallen away from the end wall of the cantina and exposed uneven courses of adobe bricks and the ends of roughly cut joists. A pair of posts supported the roof of vines which shaded the door. A few ragged mesquites and a juniper with handfuls of dark-blue berries amongst its scaly leaves grew behind the building. A burro was tethered in the shade and every now and then dipped his head to graze. Chickens pecked in the dirt and on the far side was a carefully tended kitchen garden. The track ran past the door and headed beyond the plateau towards still higher ground, the other side of which lay the border.

The cantina was a rectangular, single-roomed building, with one small window beside the door and thick walls for coolness. Inside, there were wooden benches and a few tables. On a table below the window there was a barrel of sharp wine and a collection of dusty glasses. A piece of broken mirror was propped against the wall behind the barrel. Someone had half-filled one of the glasses with water and stood a handful of bright lantana flowers in it. Out of the sunlight, in the shadowy room, their orange trumpets shone like brass. In the corner, on the earth floor, was a folded blanket beside a woven rush basket in which a baby lay asleep. A chicken had wandered in and pecked around the legs of the tables. The slab of sunlight which fell in through the open doorway sparkled with dust.

There were voices from the garden on the far side of the house, a man's and a woman's. The man was saying things to make her laugh and the sound of her laughter was carefree and contented. He was teasing her, saying she should be preparing food not picking flowers and what use were flowers inside a house when nature intended them to grow outside. Was this what she had learned to do since she had refused to come back to the village and gone to live with the gringo? Did she grow vegetables in little glasses of water inside the house too?

Wiping laughter away from her eyes, Maria came round the side of the house and ducked through the door to check on the child. She knelt on the floor beside the basket. Each breath clawed in his throat and his lips were still pale but the convulsions which had seized his lungs and pulled the colour from his cheeks had passed. She got up quietly. Luis, the owner of the cantina, stood in the doorway leaning against the lintel. His grey hair was cut short and his face was creased and weather beaten. He had followed Maria from the garden out of concern. In his cupped hands he held potatoes with the earth still clinging to them.

'He's fine,' Maria said. 'Getting better.'

'We should prepare a meal,' Luis went on. 'Lucas will be hungry when he comes.'

Maria looked away.

'He should have been here two days ago.'

Luis gestured her to follow him outside and pointed down the track which ran straight down the long slope to the desert. A distant cloud of dust showed there was a rider approaching. Maria raised her hands to her mouth to stop herself shrieking with joy. Luis shaded his eyes and stared down the track.

'He'll be an hour, maybe more.'

Luis carried a table out of the cantina and set it down in the shade of the juniper. Maria set potatoes, carrots and onions to boil over the fire and fetched an iron pan and a basket which contained four eggs from inside. As she came out of the door, she shaded her eyes and peered down the track. The dust cloud was closer but still too far away for her to identify the rider for sure.

The shade of the mesquites and the juniper together with the elevation off the desert floor made the heat of the day bearable here. The scent of the juniper leaves hung in the air and mixed with the smell of wood smoke and onions. When the vegetables were done Maria drained off the water and mashed them, mixed in red chilies, salt, broke in the eggs and set the pan over the fire again. She sang as she worked. Luis looked at her. He had sung the same old song to his own daughters years before.

'You could stay here,' he said gently. 'You and Lucas. If

127

you haven't anywhere.'

Maria smiled at him.

'You wouldn't have to pay me.'

'I have to get to my village,' Maria said.

Luis went round the front of the building to stare down the road again. A couple of minutes later he called out to her.

'You said your Lucas is a big guy, right? Tall.'

Maria went to join him and shaded her eyes again. She drew in her breath sharply.

'It's not him.'

She stepped quickly into the cantina. When she came outside again, she held the shotgun.

'Sure way to get someone to shoot at you is to carry one of those things,' Luis said.

'I know him,' Maria said. 'I know what he wants.'


'Is he coming?'

Caborca lay by the pool. The music of the falling water, the cool air and the shade of the rock walls made him want to stay there forever. If he made the slightest movement, pain stabbed his shoulder.

'He's gone.'

Lucas walked back to the pool. He patted the neck of his horse as he passed.

'What are you doing riding with him anyway?' Lucas said.

'Just picked me,' Caborca said. 'Maybe he wanted me to talk to you.'

'Picked you, made you ride with him all the way out here, then he shot you,' Lucas said. 'Don't make sense.'

'Said I wasn't going in the canyon first,' Caborca said. 'He got riled up.'

'You'll be all right. Your arm's broke that's all.'

'Told him none of the men would steal the payroll,' Caborca said. 'No one believed you'd done it.'

'What did he say?'

'It was like speaking a language he don't understand.'

'What about Hobbs?'

'Told him you ain't got it in you to kill someone. We all did.'

'He believe you about that?'

'How can you tell a guy anything if he don't want to listen?'

'You never told him what really happened?'

Caborca caught his breath as pain gouged his shoulder.

'I'm a Mexican worker,' he said. 'You think the great John Gulliver would believe anything I say?'

'We'll stay here for a day or two,' Lucas said. 'Till that arm has started to heal.'

'I want you to go on without me,' Caborca said. 'Gulliver is bound to come back. He'll kill you this time.'

Lucas smiled grimly.

'He might try but I ain't leaving you.'


Gulliver sat in the saddle and looked down at Maria. His hat, face and clothes were covered in trail dust, he was red eyed and exhausted after the ride.

'No need to point that thing at me. I ain't come to harm you.'

Maria stood in the doorway to the cantina and levelled the shot gun at his chest. Luis stood beside her.

'You ain't welcome here,' Maria said.

Inside, the baby started to cry. The distress made him catch his breath and cough. The coughing startled him and his sobbing grew loud and desperate as his frustration flared into rage. His screams stifled the rattle of air which clawed his lungs. Maria lowered the shot gun and went inside.

Gulliver climbed down off his horse.

'Just want a drink of water, mister,' Gulliver said. 'I've rode a long way.'

It took Gulliver a moment to get used to the dark room after the sunlight outside. He missed his footing on the uneven floor and grabbed at the edge of the table inside the door. The rows of glasses clinked like a handful of change and one which held a posy toppled and fell. Water ran into a pool on the table and the flowers rolled on to the floor.

Maria sat on a bench at the far end of the cantina with the shotgun across her knees. She held the child at her shoulder, soothed his back and whispered softly in his ear. He had stopped crying but each breath tore his lungs. Gulliver sat down near the door and turned to Luis.

'Fetch me a pitcher of water.'

He leaned back against the wall. His jacket fell aside and showed a silver Colt in its holster.

'And take care of the horse.'

Luis fetched a clay jug filled with water and a glass from the table by the door, set them down beside Gulliver and went outside again. Gulliver turned to Maria.

'Knew I'd find you here.'

The child had cried himself out. Maria laid him in the basket and he coughed again then stayed calm even though the breath still rattled in his throat. She set down the shotgun and, without looking at Gulliver, crossed the room and stooped to pick up the lantanas and set them in the glass. She took Gulliver's water jug and tipped a little into the glass. Then she sat back down beside the baby and replaced the shotgun on her lap.

'When are you expecting him?' Gulliver said.

Maria looked down at the child. His eyes were closed and the redness caused by his screaming had left his face.

'Today?' Gulliver continued. 'Tomorrow? Maybe something's happened. You thought about that?'

Maria refused to look at him.

'Sheriff's on his trail, I can tell you that.' Gulliver said. 'Maybe he's caught up with him.'

He paused.

'Maybe he ain't coming at all.'

Maria's hands moved over the shotgun on her lap. Gulliver's words hung in the air between them.

'I'm just saying,' Gulliver said.

Dust danced in the sunlight in front of the doorway. A little brown lizard popped its head out from behind one of the benches, skittered out into the centre of the room and froze. He cocked his head to one side then the other and skittered back again leaving a trail in the dust. From round the back of the cantina came the sound of Luis talking gently in Spanish to Gulliver's horse.

'Sheriff could have caught up with him. Could have him under arrest right now,' Gulliver went on.

'Shut up,' Maria said.

Gulliver laughed, pleased with himself for having goaded a response from her.

'Can't blame the sheriff. He's a lawman just doing his job. If your husband's broke the law, well. . . .'

Gulliver spread his hands.

'Lucas is a good man,' Maria said.

'Listen,' Gulliver said. 'He killed my manager, stole the payroll and he ran off to meet you at the border.'

Luis slipped in through the door, took the piece of

131

broken mirror from behind the wine barrel and went out again. Gulliver barely noticed him.

'If he's wanted for murdering a man, that's the sheriff's business. If he's took my money, that's mine.'

'How many more times?' Maria said. 'Lucas just wouldn't do that.'

'You're wrong,' Gulliver snarled. 'Money's gone. He's headed for the border.'

Maria's hands closed over the trigger guard.

There was a shout from outside. Luis was calling to them.

'Someone's coming.'

Maria and Gulliver leapt to their feet.

Way beyond the bottom of the slope on the desert floor, a cloud of brown dust was kicked up by a horse. Gulliver looked at Maria.

'Didn't think he'd make it.'

Maria strained to see. Was it Lucas? The glare of the sun off the hard ground stung her eyes.

'Couple of hours,' Luis said. 'Hour and a half maybe.'

'When he gets here, all he's got to do is hand over my money,' Gulliver said. 'He can take his chances making a run for the border with the sheriff after him.'

'He won't have your money,' Maria said stubbornly.

'Tell you one thing,' Gulliver said. 'He rides off to the border with you and that kid slowing him down, sheriff is sure to catch him. If he takes off without you, the bandits the other side of that hill will kill him first time they see him.'

'I asked you once already,' Birkmeir said.

Blood dribbled down Jackson's chin. He tried to say something but the words slipped round his swollen mouth.

'What?'

Birkmeir screwed up his face in the effort to understand.

'Ain't done nothing, Sheriff.'

'Hell you ain't,' Birkmeir said. 'Trouble follows you like a shadow.'

'Take these cuffs off, Sheriff.'

'Last time you was in Ponderosa, your boys bust up the saloon so bad, Charlie practically had to rebuild the place. If I hadn't been outa town, they would have ended up behind bars. None of you ain't paid a red cent in compensation.'

'Sheriff,' Jackson protested. 'Just take the cuffs off. I can't be held for what my boys does.'

Birkmeir ignored him.

'You're wanted in Los Angeles for robbing a bank. There's a price on your head,' Birkmeir said. 'You ain't told me what you're doing out here anyhow.'

'Nothing, Sheriff,' Jackson pleaded. 'Just needed a place to rest up for a while.'

'No one comes out here to rest up. Hide maybe, if they're on the run.'

Birkmeir looked Jackson in the eye.

'You and your boys done a robbery out on the coast, come to the desert to hole up till they give up looking for you?'

'Sheriff, I'm telling you.'

'What have you got in your saddle-bags?'

Birkmeir left him leaning against the post and walked over to where his horse was tethered in the shade. He flicked open the laces and brought out the bank bag.

'What's this?'

'That's mine, Sheriff. I earned it.'

133

Birkmeir laughed.

'Earned it?'

'Playing poker,' Jackson said.

'Against who, your grandmother?'

Birkmeir glared at him.

'You can't prove nothing,' Jackson spluttered.

'Let's get this straight,' Birkmeir said. 'You're sitting out here at Red Tail all on your own with a bag full of money. That means you've done a robbery. Most likely with your boys seeing as how you've brought them up to be outlaws.'

'Sheriff,' Jackson said.

'Shut up. Seeing as how you ain't gonna tell me the truth, I've got to work it out for myself.' Birkmeir followed his train of thought. 'Probably means your boys are gonna meet you here. Then what are you going to do?'

'Sheriff,' Jackson insisted. 'My boys is dead.'

Birkmeir looked at him.

'Lucas Redwood shot 'em both and stole their money.'

# 14

'Give me that shotgun,' Gulliver snapped. 'I ain't having you waving that thing about.'

He pushed past Maria, strode into the cantina and snatched the gun from beside the baby. Maria made a grab for it but he shoved her away. As he broke open the breech, two shells tumbled into the child's basket.

'All he's got to do is give me my money,' Gulliver said. 'Seeing you with that thing might put ideas in his head.'

'You got your story wrong,' Maria said wearily. 'I told you.'

She leaned down and smoothed the cotton sheet over the child. Gulliver pocketed the shells and stood the gun in a corner of the room.

Outside, they shaded their eyes and peered at the approaching figure. The heat was building and his progress was slow.

'There's two of 'em,' Gulliver said.

Maria stared hard through the dust and glassy air.

'It ain't him,' she said.

Two riders emerged out of the heat. One was upright in the saddle, the other leaned to the side as if he was in pain.

'Where's the Mexican?' Gulliver said.

'Luis?' Maria said. 'He was just here.'

When the riders were half way up the slope, Gulliver recognized them. He brought a bench out of the cantina, placed it against the wall and sat down to check his Colt. He spun the chamber. The mechanism was oiled and ready, six shells in place.

Seeing him unholster his gun, Maria went inside and stayed with the child. She pulled the door shut behind her. Gulliver checked behind the building, expecting to find Luis tending his garden but there was no one. His horse and the burro stood in the shade of the juniper.

Sheriff Birkmeir led Jackson's horse. Jackson's hands were tied behind his back. With his gun loose in its holster, Gulliver leaned back against the wall and watched Birkmeir dismount.

'Lucas here?' Birkmeir said. 'Reckoned he might still be in the canyon so we came the long way.'

He brushed the dust off his clothes.

'Not yet,' Gulliver said. 'Got his wife and kid inside.'

He called out to Maria to bring a jug of water. Birkmeir pulled Jackson out of the saddle and steadied him so he didn't fall.

'You could take these things off me,' Jackson said. His swollen mouth blurred his words.

'If you wasn't cuffed,' Birkmeir said, 'I'd need a forked stick.'

He shoved Jackson over to the bench.

'This one's got something to tell you,' Birkmeir said.

Maria pushed open the door balancing a jug of water and glasses. The sheriff nodded a greeting to her.

'I'll tell you,' Jackson said. 'But you've got to let me go.'

'Got to?' Birkmeir sneered.

'John junior and Lucas stole some silver bars and was

136

selling it to my boys,' Jackson began. 'The deal went bad and the only one who survived was Lucas. He shot 'em all.'

The glasses rattled as Maria set them down in front of the men.

'You expect me to believe that?' Gulliver said.

'Bodies is in the shaft at Red Tail along with the silver.'

'John junior is running the smelting works,' Gulliver snapped. 'He'll inherit the whole company. He don't need to sell anything.'

'Another thing.' Birkmeir poured himself a glass of water and nodded at Jackson. 'He just happens to have a San Francisco bank-bag full of money with him.'

'I told you I won that money,' Jackson protested. 'You gotta take these cuffs off me.'

The sheriff unholstered his Colt and pointed it at Jackson.

'Long enough for you to take a drink. Then I'm putting 'em back on.'

He took a key out of his pocket.

'Maybe Lucas had something on John junior,' Jackson suggested.

'Gave my son everything he needed,' Gulliver snapped. 'His whole life was mapped out.'

Jackson drank the water greedily with Birkmeir's gun aimed at his chest.

'My boys found their own way,' Jackson said. 'Didn't make no difference in the end.'

'Enough,' Gulliver snapped. 'Put the cuffs back on him.'

Two hours later, Lucas and Pablo Caborca emerged from the heat haze and climbed the slope up to the cantina. Maria's heart leapt as she recognized them. Gulliver and the others had their hats pulled down over their faces and were dozing in the heat. She stepped back inside the cantina to give herself time to think. Should she try and get down the slope to warn him? She might be able to find a way through the trees. Should she wait until he was nearer and call out? Where was Luis? Why had he disappeared now when he could have helped her? She looked at the sleeping child. Each breath was light and rattled in his chest. Lucas would want her to stay with him.

Then there was movement outside. She heard Gulliver's voice. They had spotted the riders. She picked up the child and held him close. He murmured at her without opening his eyes. It was too late to do anything now. She opened the door and sunlight blinded her for a moment. Gulliver and the others stared down the track. Lucas rode straight towards them, he had seen them and quickened his pace.

Maria pushed past the men, out into the track. She had not intended to but there was a lightness in her step as she turned and began to run down the hill. Someone shouted behind her. Maria screamed out a warning as she ran. Just his name, just the one word as loud as she could. Gulliver dodged in front of her and grabbed her throat. His grip tightened like a claw until she thought he might tear out her windpipe. She struggled to hold on to the child. Gulliver shouted something but blood pounded in her ears and deafened her. Over his shoulder she could see Lucas riding towards them.

Gulliver's gun was in his other hand.

'Get back inside,' he snarled.

The child kicked out, struggled for air and sobbed. Each breath convulsed him. Gulliver let go of her throat, grabbed her arm and dragged her back towards the cantina. A rifle shot cracked somewhere; the bullet whined through the air. Gulliver dropped her arm and started to run. Maria followed him. There was another shot. She heard the bullet rip into the trees. The child was screaming now, screaming and gulping air as if he was drowning. At the top of the rise, beyond the cantina a line of men blocked the road. Luis was amongst them and held a Winchester at his shoulder.

Maria flung herself in through the door.

'Bandits from over the border,' Gulliver said. 'How did they find out we was here?'

'They come for Lucas?' Birkmeir said. 'Or us?'

Gulliver turned to Maria.

'You did this.'

Maria paced the room hoping the motion would calm the child. His tiny lungs heaved in and out as he gulped each breath. All her concentration was on him, listening for the smallest change in his crying, the slightest settling of his breath.

'You told that Mexican to fetch the bandits.'

'Luis?' Maria said. 'How could I? I've been with you all the time.'

'Before,' Gulliver snapped. 'It must have been you.'

'Can't you stop that kid crying?' Jackson said.

Usually, the thick walls made the cantina retain some coolness even in the heat of the day but with them all inside and the door closed the place was airless.

'Can't you put him outside?' Jackson said.

Maria glared at him. The child cried out as if each breath scorched his lungs.

'What do they want?' Birkmeir said. 'Whatever it is, we better give it to them or we ain't worth a nickel.'

'What did you tell them?' Gulliver insisted. 'You send a

139

message about Lucas having the payroll so he could buy a way across?'

The child screamed in agony. His lips were lines of ivory. Maria stared at his face and rocked him back and forth.

'Everyone knows those bandits won't let anyone through,' Gulliver went on.

Maria watched Gulliver calculate how he could use her. He turned to Birkmeir.

'Take Jackson's cuffs off. We need him on our side now.'

'That's right,' Jackson said. 'You need me.'

Gulliver nodded to Maria.

'Put the kid down,' he said. 'Put him in the basket. Then take him outside. You're no use to us in here.'

'I didn't tell them to come,' Maria said nervously. 'I don't know what they want.'

Gulliver waved his Colt at her.

'That husband of yours is out there. Don't you want to be with him?'

Maria placed the child in the basket and folded a sheet over him. As she stood up, Gulliver grabbed her arms and wrenched them behind her until the joints cracked. Taken by surprise, she screamed and struggled and although she was strong his thin fingers bit into her wrists.

'Bring the cuffs,' he yelled to Birkmeir.

Gulliver wrestled Maria across the room, kicked open the door, twisted her arms behind her back, one each side of the porch post while the sheriff locked the handcuffs on her. Jackson seized the basket and the screaming baby, carried it out and dumped it beside her. The men ducked back inside.

'They ain't gonna shoot with her there,' Gulliver said. 'Buys us some time.'

140

'Did you see 'em?'

'Still lined up across the track,' Jackson said. 'Five or six of 'em, walking down the hill. Didn't seem in no hurry.'

'How many of 'em are armed?' Gulliver said.

'All of 'em.'

'Did you see Lucas?'

'Track was clear. Either high tailed it or dived off into the trees.'

'Best wait till dark,' Gulliver said, 'Then you can make a break for it. Won't be no trouble getting away, those Mexicans ain't got horses.'

'What about you?' Birkmeir said.

'Staying with the woman,' Gulliver said. 'Lucas will come for her. I came here to kill him and take back the payroll.'

The men took turns keeping watch at the window. Glad of something to do at last, Jackson was first. He could see the back of Maria's head against the porch post and beyond her across the track into the trees. The track which led up the hill where the Mexicans were and down towards where they had seen Lucas was out of his range of vision. Every now and then, one of the Mexicans called out either some insult to the men in the cantina or something in Spanish to Maria. Maria spoke constantly to the child and eventually he settled again and slept. Gulliver was right, with Maria handcuffed to the post there was no more shooting.

The heat and the airless room sapped the men's strength. They leaned back against the walls and tried to rest.

'Believe me yet?' Jackson said to Gulliver. 'That I didn't kill your boy?'

'Don't believe nothing he says,' Birkmeir interrupted.

141

'He's a wanted man. I've known Lucas ever since I've been sheriff of Ponderosa.'

'I gave my son everything,' Gulliver said. 'You're telling me he stole what belonged to him?'

The men passed round a pitcher of water and drained it.

Outside, Maria slid down the post so she could sit on the ground. She could look over the edge of the basket and watch the face of her sleeping child. The vision of his tiny face absorbed her just as it always did. She noticed everything, the damp strands of hair across his forehead, the lift of his eyelashes, the little bubbles at his lips, the perfect curve of his beautiful mouth. She heard every breath enter his lungs. Even when he was peaceful, there was always a seed of anxiety in her in case the rattle in his chest made him catch his breath and cough. There were even moments when she forgot where she was, that her hands were tied, that if there was shooting she was in the line of fire.

As the air cooled, shadows filled the spaces between the trees. A sudden movement in the undergrowth caught Maria's attention and startled her. Some animal maybe. Her throat was parched but she preferred to suffer than ask for a drink. The men who had tied her here were cowards beneath contempt.

Then there was another rustle and the undergrowth was pushed aside: a buck mule deer popped his head out between the trees and stared straight at Maria. A crown of antlers towered over his huge, velvet ears. His white nose and bib were luminous against the shadows. He stood perfectly still and his gaze was unflinching. He had come for the juniper behind the cantina but as she was there, decided against it, turned and trotted a few yards down

142

the hill. Then with effortless muscular grace, he sprang into the undergrowth again and was gone.

Maria could hear the voices of those cowards inside the cantina. They would be wanting to run away now it was getting dark. How much longer did they intend to leave her out here? When the child woke, she would have to feed him. They would have to release her. She rested her head back against the post. Thirst clawed her throat and her mouth tasted of sand. She concentrated on the undergrowth opposite. Were there more deer in there? Something moved, she was sure of it. The child's breathing quickened slightly and Maria's eyes flicked to him.

Maria's scream erupted from deep inside her. She pushed herself up the post so she was standing again. Splinters tore into her back. She carried on screaming and her screams ripped her throat. Someone shouted inside the cantina and then the other men started talking. She heard one of them say something about a trick and Gulliver's voice yelling at them not to go out there. She heard them at the window behind her head. And she couldn't stop. Her agonized cry ruptured her throat and lungs until her chest burned. She hammered the cuffs again and again into the post desperate for the chain to break. The steel chafed the skin of her wrists until her hands were wet and she knew it was blood. Then she realized, if her hands were wet she could slip one of them through the cuffs. She heaved her two hands against the steel and felt the metal shave her wrists to the bone.

The diamond camouflage along the back of the rattler was greenish-grey, its pebble head was smooth as jet and the end of its tail was ringed and pale. It slid around the body of the sleeping child, curled into an s-shape and raised its head. Its black tongue flicked to taste the air.

Wrists slippery with blood, Maria heaved against the cuffs until her strength failed and her scream tortured her throat until it was hoarse. Then there was an explosion behind the line of trees.

Lucas's huge frame burst through the undergrowth. He crashed through the creosote bushes and sprang towards her over the track, his axe in his right hand. There was a yell from the cantina window. Lucas glanced in the basket and flashed a look into Maria's eyes. He took a pace behind her, swung the axe and with a single blow split the steel handcuffs apart. Maria staggered forward.

Holding the axe by the blade, the polished shaft out in front of him, Lucas stepped towards the basket. Commotion raged inside the cantina; Gulliver yelled. Lucas gently smoothed the shaft under the body of the snake. It turned its head to inspect him and its tongue flicked. Lucas eased the shaft further. The child stirred. The rattler swiveled its head to look. Lucas lifted the shaft of the axe and the greenback hung down on either side, still supporting his head and scrutinizing the air around him, unperturbed because of the lightness of the movement. Lucas crossed the track and lowered him amongst the creosote bushes.

There was a shout from the doorway of the cantina. Gulliver's voice. As Lucas turned, a pistol shot cracked. Lucas staggered, dropped his axe and fell backwards on to the dusty track.

# 15

Maria threw herself down beside Lucas, whispered in his ear and held his face. She lifted his hand away from his side where his shirt was soaked in blood. There were shouts behind her. Birkmeir and Jackson tumbled out of the cantina. There was more shouting further up the track. Then Pablo Caborca was there kneeling on the other side of Lucas's body, his arm strapped up in a filthy bandage, speaking softly to him. Maria slid Lucas's gun from his belt and slipped it into the pocket of her skirt.

'Is he dead?'

It was Gulliver's voice.

Maria flung herself at him and smashed a storm of punches at his face. Gulliver reeled. As he raised his arms to protect himself, his gun fell to the ground. Maria saw it and made a grab, but Birkmeir kicked it away, seized her arm and twisted it behind her back. She struggled as pain skewered her shoulder. Jackson grabbed Maria's other arm. Gulliver stepped back and wiped the blood away from his mouth.

Pablo Caborca helped Lucas up. His face was twisted and blood ran through his fingers where he held his great hand over the wound in his side. Jackson handed Gulliver his gun. For a second he pointed it at Lucas then noticed Luis and a group of half a dozen men advancing down the hill.

'Back inside,' Gulliver snapped.

As they turned, they saw the torches. At the foot of the incline, there were thirty of them, forty maybe. An army of men marching up from the desert carried flaming torches through the gathering dusk. The sight stunned them. Behind them, Luis and the Mexicans stood still and were staring too.

'Bandits?' Jackson said.

'There are no bandits,' Maria snapped.

Jackson looked back up the slope. Luis had lowered his rifle, his eyes fixed on the advancing men. Maria nodded towards them.

'They are farmers. They defend themselves when gringos cross the border to steal their cattle.'

'Let her go,' Gulliver said to Birkmeir. 'It don't look good.'

Maria wrenched her arm free. Jackson made no attempt to hold her. She crossed the track to Lucas. She and Caborca helped him over to the bench by the cantina wall.

They could all hear the tramp of feet now as the band of men advanced up the hill. Luis made his way down to the cantina, the men with him had hurried back towards the border. Everyone's eyes were on the tide of torchlight which flowed towards them.

Gulliver stood in front of Lucas. His gun was holstered but his hand hovered over it.

'You got my money?' he said. 'That's what I come for.'

Lucas looked at him. Pain drained his face.

'The payroll,' Gulliver prompted.

Maria started forward at him again. Lucas held her back.

'We ain't got time for this,' Gulliver said.

Jackson and Birkmeir stared down the hill.

'Who are they?' Jackson said. 'Ain't no use in barricading ourselves inside. Too many of 'em.'

'What do they want?' Birkmeir said.

Gulliver's hand rested on his Colt. He leaned towards Lucas.

'You gonna give me what's mine?' he hissed. 'Or am I gonna have to shoot you again?'

'Ain't got your payroll,' Lucas said. 'Never had it.'

Pain made his voice small and tight in his mouth. Gulliver unholstered his gun and jabbed it in Lucas's gut.

'You're lyin',' Gulliver snapped. 'You ran off.'

'I told him to.' Caborca stepped between Lucas and Gulliver. 'It was an accident. Hobbs grabbed me by the throat and Lucas pushed him off me. He fell against the cabin wall, cracked the back of his head.'

'You—' Gulliver spat.

Luis jabbed Gulliver in the small of his back with the barrel of his Winchester.

'You gonna shoot one of your men in front of all these others?'

Gulliver wheeled round. In the torchlight, he could see the men's faces now and recognized some of them from the charcoal camp. Out in front were Wheeling and Tucker, the foremen he had left in charge, their hands tied behind them. Gulliver slid his gun back into its holster.

'What's going on?'

There was a shout from someone in the crowd who recognized Lucas. Maria smiled as the men called her

147

husband's name. She gathered up the sleeping baby and held him in her arms. Caborca called out to the men.

'You hurt, Lucas?' Henry Meadows pushed through the crowd.

'Reckon I bust a rib,' Lucas said. 'Hopin' the bullet passed through.'

'Who did it?' Meadows said.

'He stole the payroll,' Gulliver said. 'That's why I came out here.'

'You mean this?'

Meadows reached into his pocket and brought out an empty canvas bag with the bank's name stencilled on the side. Gulliver snatched it.

'Where did you get this?'

Meadows jerked his thumb at the foremen.

'They hid it.'

Gulliver peered at Tucker and Wheeling.

'You stole it?'

They stared at the ground.

'Sounds like an admission of guilt,' Birkmeir said.

Gulliver looked round at Lucas.

'You were telling the truth?' Disbelief echoed in his voice. He caught Caborca's eye. 'You're saying it was an accident?'

Caborca nodded.

'They said you was going to can us,' Meadows said.

The men behind him fell silent.

'Bring in Chinese workers from San Francisco and pay 'em half what you pay us.'

Gulliver hesitated.

'Business ain't making enough profit,' he said. 'Now the treeline is cut back so far, it takes too long to drag the lumber down to the kilns. Kilns are being fired half empty,

148

the whole process is too slow.'

'You sayin' we worked ourselves out of a job?' someone called out. 'You wouldn't can us if we hadn't cut back so much timber?'

'It ain't that—' Gulliver began.

'We ain't going to allow it,' Meadows interrupted, 'whatever the reason. We ain't going to let you can us and we ain't going to let you pay those Chinese fellas less than what's fair. You're a rich man.'

'I'm the boss,' Gulliver roared. 'That's something you'll never be.'

Meadows stepped backwards. In the flickering torch-light, rage burned in Gulliver's face.

'What do you think, Lucas?' Meadows said. 'You with us?'

' 'Course you're right,' Lucas said. 'But I ain't working for no one no more.'

'What are you gonna do?' Gulliver sneered. 'Scratch in the dirt alongside the other sodbusters?'

Anger swelled the muttered conversations in the crowd.

Lucas looked at Gulliver calmly. His hand protected the wound in his side.

'I got enough money for us to make a new start, help my wife's family, if we go where the living is cheap.'

Gulliver rounded on him.

'You must have stole it,' he yelled. 'You can't make enough for a new start felling timber. I knew it. You almost had me fooled.'

He slashed his arm through the air towards the others.

'All of you, covering for him, covering for each other.'

'I did a job and got paid for it,' Lucas said.

'You're one of my cutters,' Gulliver screamed. 'Nothing more.'

149

Maria held the child close. His breathing caught in his throat again.

'I did a job for your son,' Lucas persisted. 'He wanted me to keep quiet about it so he paid well.'

Pain tightened his breath.

'Took silver up to Red Tail. He was selling it on.'

Gulliver stared at him.

'John junior?'

'Hired me to take silver from the wagon outside the smelting works up to Red Tail.'

'It was all his,' Gulliver said.

Gulliver's face was stone. It betrayed nothing, no sign of grief, no regret, no emotion. The fury which burned within him was invisible and he stood ready for a trigger to release his rage. His hand tightened on the handle of his .45.

'None of that matters now,' Lucas said. 'Got in a gun-fight. They all died. Him included. Bodies are in the old mineshaft along with the silver.'

'That's what I told the sheriff,' Jackson said. 'My sons too.'

Gulliver said nothing.

'You and him need to get up to Red Tail to see 'em buried proper,' Birkmeir said.

'Joe McCall's with 'em,' Lucas said.

'McCall?' Gulliver sneered. 'He was weak. Did whatever I said for years. Somebody must have pushed him into it.'

'Tried to strike out on his own,' Lucas said. 'Left it too late and didn't make it.'

Gulliver stood surrounded by the men. His contempt for them was palpable. They had explained things to him but he hadn't understood. He looked into their faces but couldn't read them. He was unlike them. He was the boss.

His son was dead and they could never understand what that meant because his son was the boss's son, heir to the empire.

'What happened to the payroll money?' Gulliver said.

'Every man took his share,' Meadows said.

'Your last pay from me,' Gulliver said. 'I rode out there to tell you I was closing the camp, replacing the work-force.'

He turned to Lucas.

'And you,' he said. 'If the sheriff ain't going to arrest you, I am.'

'He never stole nothing,' Birkmeir said. 'Never killed no one.'

'You're the sheriff,' Gulliver said. 'I'm telling you to arrest him.'

Birkmeir looked him in the eye.

'I've paid off the rest of you,' Gulliver went on. 'You ain't nothing to me now.'

'We ain't going to let you do this,' Meadows said. 'We've decided. We'll take over the camp. We'll give you a fair price for the acreage. If you want to buy charcoal after that, we can negotiate a fair price for that too.'

'What?' Gulliver screamed. 'You can't afford to buy it.'

'Not me,' Meadows said. 'All of us together.'

Gulliver wheeled from the crowd of men to face Lucas and back again.

'Seems fair to me,' Birkmeir said.

'Fair?' Gulliver yelled. 'There ain't no such thing as fair.'

He drew his gun then and jabbed it at Lucas.

'If the sheriff ain't going to arrest you, I gotta deal with you myself.'

He cocked the hammer. There was shouting amongst

the men. Birkmeir and Jackson both yelled. Luis grabbed the Winchester he had propped by the door but he was too late. A pistol shot cracked.

Gulliver toppled forward. Maria cradled the child in her left arm and held Lucas's pistol in her right hand. Smoke rose from the barrel. The men surged forward. Birkmeir kicked Gulliver's gun aside. Luis put down his rifle. Maria handed the Colt to Lucas and sank down on the bench beside him. A pool of blood spread from under Gulliver's body. Birkmeir knelt down and laid two fingers against the side of his neck. A moment later, he looked up at Maria and shook his head.

# 16

Sheriff Birkmeir paid Luis to guard Tucker and Wheeling overnight. Jackson laid out his bed-roll on the porch of the cantina while Lucas, Maria and the child bedded down inside. The men built fires and slept on the verges of the track and at times during the night movement of mule deer amongst the trees woke them briefly. As dawn broke, the cool air smelled of coffee and wood-smoke.

Maria had torn up a shirt belonging to Luis and bound Lucas's ribs. Although the bandage quickly crusted with blood, the slightest movement pained him. He lay still all night.

Luis wrapped Gulliver's body into a sheet and sewed it fast. He helped Jackson heave it over the saddle of his horse.

'That story true about the bodies in the old shaft at Red Tail?' Luis said.

'Every word,' Jackson said. 'Headed there now to bury my boys decent.'

'True about the silver too?'

Jackson looked at him. 'Sheriff ain't gonna let me keep that.'

'Reckon you've got a lot of buryin' to do,' Luis contin-

153

ued. 'Your boys, Gulliver, the others. Pay me and I'll help you.'

'You're willing to help me?' Jackson said.

'I work, you pay me,' Luis said. 'You've been double crossin' so long, you've forgotton what that's like, ain't you?'

Henry Meadows pressed Lucas to come and work with him and the others when they took over the charcoal camp. Lucas sat on the floor of the cantina and leant against the wall. His pale face was covered with a film of sweat.

'Rest up,' Meadows said. 'Get your strength back, then come over. All the fellas want you to be part of it.'

Lucas shook his head.

'Appreciate you coming out here to speak for me,' he said. 'You and all the guys.'

He caught Maria's eye.

'Maria's family, all the people in her village are poorer than you'll ever be this side of the border. I got the chance to do something for them.'

Maria gently dabbed a cotton cloth over his forehead.

'If you ever change your mind. . . .' Meadows said.

'We're gonna stay here till I can ride, then we'll head down there.'

Pablo Caborca pushed open the cantina door.

'Brought the horses up from where we hid 'em in the brush last night.'

A heavy saddle-bag was looped over his good arm. He dropped it beside Lucas. Meadows turned to him.

'Comin' back with us?' Meadows said. 'Sure need guys like you.'

'Come from the same village as Maria,' Caborca said. 'Only crossed the border to work so I could send money home. I'll ride back with them.'

'Same applies,' Meadows said. 'Ever feel like coming back, there'll be a place for you.'

From outside came the sounds of men's voices. They had rolled up their blankets and doused the fires. The sky was pale in the east and the orange sun pushed above the horizon.

'If we leave now we'll get to Freshwater by midday,' Meadows said. 'Rest up there while the afternoon burns itself out. Start walking again this evening.'

Luis gave Maria instructions about keeping the garden watered and tied a pick and shovels on to his saddle.

Lucas insisted Maria and Pablo Caborca help him to his feet so he could walk outside and see the men leave. Maria stood beside him, holding the child. Lucas leaned against the wall of the cantina and, to his surprise, when they saw him there all forty of the men insisted on filing past him; each of them clasped his hand and wished him luck. Meadows was last in line.

'Don't forget what I said,' he said and grasped Lucas by the arm.

Laughter echoed through the trees as the men strode down the track. Tucker and Wheeling were roped together by the wrist and followed the column. Birkmeir rode behind them. Jackson and Luis, leading Gulliver's horse, were last.

Lucas waited until the column was out of sight and then sat down on the bench. Maria placed the child in the crook of his powerful arm, away from the wound. She went back inside the cantina and soon Lucas heard the gentle sound of her sweeping. The child's cheeks were flushed, every breath rattled in his chest and forced his lungs to overwork.

After a few minutes, Maria came out of the cantina,

propped her brush against the wall and sat beside them while Caborca inspected Luis's garden round the side of the building.

'I counted the money,' Maria said.

Lucas continued to stare at the child.

'You could help the men with that.'

'The men are working together,' Lucas said. 'They'll always be able to sell their timber.'

He turned to Maria.

'The money's for us,' Lucas said. 'For your family and the village.'

Lucas looked down into the face of the child again.

'And for him.'

Lucas stayed there most of the morning, watching the child sleep. Maria and Caborca tidied the cantina, collected the eggs, fed the horses and the burro and searched out weeds in Luis's neat garden. She picked handfuls of epazote and boiled up a poisonous smelling tea for soaking Lucas's bandages. In the heat of the day, Maria took the child and, having dressed Lucas's wounds again, spread his bed-roll on the porch for him so he could sleep.

When the afternoon gave way to evening, Maria built a fire, killed one of Luis's chickens and boiled it with onions from the garden. But Lucas was feverish and refused food. He wouldn't move from his blanket on the porch and lay for hours in a state of semi-wakefulness. As the fever returned, she began to doubt that the bullet had passed through him and dread seized her that it was still lodged beneath his ribs and the wound would go bad. Eventually Lucas agreed to Maria changing his dressing again. She tore up an old sheet and soaked it in the epazote water.

A bruise covered the left side of Lucas's ribs, livid and overripe. Maria looked for yellowness around the wound,

156

but there was little swelling and the hole made by the bullet was clean. Even though it pained him, she insisted Lucas lean forward while she looked for the exit wound to satisfy herself and found it had begun to heal. Later, while Lucas slept, she took a torch from the fire and examined the trees at the edge of the track opposite the house and found a bullet buried in the trunk of one of the mesquites.

The days went on like this. Maria nursed Lucas, changed his dressings and washed out his bandages in whatever herbal concoctions she could make. She bandaged Pablo Caborca's arm; she saw to the child; she cooked for them all. Caborca helped where he could.

When Lucas woke on the morning of the fourth day, his fever was gone. He was weak but his eyes were clear and he was hungry. Maria made him broth from chicken bones.

Late in the morning, Luis rode up the track. He had a sack of white beans, a bag of seed potatoes and a wooden cage containing three hens tied to his saddle. The money Jackson had paid him would last all summer, he said. He described the line of graves they had dug on the ridge above the Red Tail Saloon and how they had made markers with cottonwood boards cut from the saloon wall. They had laid Gulliver beside his son and Jackson's two boys together. Joe McCall was between them. Luis had wanted Jackson to say words over the graves but all he said was they had been men who made their choices and lived by them and that was all any of us could expect.

That evening Luis built up the fire and cooked beans, onions and wild garlic and flavoured it with some of Maria's epazote leaves. He brought glasses and his barrel of wine out on to the porch. Luis himself was content to slug back his wine as he stirred the beans with a wooden spoon, but the sharpness was too much for the others.

Lucas had emerged from his fever, his brain busy with ideas about what they would do when they got to Maria's village. The first thing was to pay for a doctor to visit once a month he said. Those who could pay would and those who were too poor would be paid for by him or the others. He would build a house on Maria's family's land, a strong brickhouse with wooden floors. He would buy a stallion and a breeding mare. He would sell the foals at the market in San Vicente and little by little the farm would become a ranch and provide work for everyone.

Maria, Caborca and Luis became caught up in Lucas's description of the place.

'I could plant lemon trees,' Maria said. 'And apricots and vines.'

'I would work hard at a place like that,' Pablo Caborca said. 'Maybe I could build a house in the village too.'

'Now that I have the money to get started,' Lucas said, 'Everything is possible.'

'These vines,' Luis reflected. 'How much do you know about vines? I could come and help you there. I've been making wine for. . . .' He swayed slightly and drew in the air with his spoon. 'I don't know how long.'

The others laughed and clinked glasses with him.

That night, Maria lay close to Lucas and rested her head on his shoulder. The child's breathing had settled and moonlight filled the window. Luis snored gently out on the porch.

'Could we really have a place like that?' Maria whispered. 'Somewhere everyone can share in?'

Lucas turned his head towards her. He reached over and brushed her dark hair back from her face. Before he could lean over to kiss her, her eyes had closed and she was asleep.

# ONE YEAR LATER

The queue began to form at first light. An orderly line of men, women and children waited outside the white painted brick house where Maria's cousin lived. Inside, the young doctor from San Vicente was holding his monthly surgery. The doctor's visits were the envy of the neighbourhood: he had completed his training at medical school in Madrid and carried all the latest equipment with him in a leather case. This included a device which enabled him to listen not just to the beating of the human heart but to the breath entering and leaving the lungs, the sound of life itself.

The doctor's manner was brusque and kindly and the carefulness with which he considered what his patients told him inspired their confidence. Some of the villagers held a few coins in their hands to pay for their treatment, others would repay Lucas by helping him to build his new house.

Inside, a child lay on a wooden table while the doctor listened to his breathing through a polished wood tube with a brass bell at one end, which rested on the patient's chest, and a smaller bell at the other on which the doctor placed his ear. Maria stood beside him trying not to let anxiety show in her face.

The doctor stood up and smiled at her.

'It's the good air,' he said. 'Being on higher ground, the air is clearer than it was in the desert. Every time I come, the asthma is a little better.'

'He's well, doctor,' Maria said. 'His breathing rarely troubles him in the night.'

Maria slipped a shirt back on to the child.

'He'll grow out of it,' the doctor continued. 'You brought him to the right place.'

The doctor placed the stethoscope back in his bag.

Maria left the surgery and carried the child to the outskirts of the village to where Lucas and Pablo Caborca were working. One leg of the L-shaped design was almost complete. The roof was on and the walls awaited their coat of finishing mud plaster. Row on row of bricks were laid out to dry beside a stack of timber. In the centre of what would be the courtyard, a well was partially dug. Beside it was a lemon tree, still only a foot high.

Lucas and Caborca looked up from their work filling the wooden brick frames with mud as Maria approached.

'The doctor says we did the right thing coming here,' Maria called. 'The asthma will disappear over time.'

A little way from where the men were working, a roan stallion stood in his coral. The horse walked expectantly towards Maria as she approached. Maria patted his neck, and spoke softly in his ear. Lucas came and stood beside her, lifted the child from her arms, slipped his arm round Maria's shoulder and drew her close. The horse's ears moved to catch the voices from the doctor's queue and the steady slap of Pablo Caborca trowelling mud into the line of wooden frames for more bricks. Then the stallion pulled away from them and broke into a sudden gallop round the coral, kicked out his legs and reared up to show off his strength in the new daylight and the clear morning air.